P9-CCY-043

My mother had a different way of doing things.

Officially, this is my fourth day in captivity. I have started keeping tally on the back of that dumb hero sign. One good thing, though. Mrs. Murphy has cleared some time to take me clothes shopping. In an actual store.

This is a far cry from my mother and I making late-night visits to Salvation Army drop boxes to "shop." I remember how she'd hand me a flashlight, hoist me into the bins, and then make requests for sizes and specific colors like I was sitting in there with a doting saleslady and a catalog.

It was cool, though, how we'd go to McDonald's afterward and my mother would hold up her ice cream as if to toast me. "Carley, what would I do without you?" she'd ask.

Back when I was little, I used to wonder why there weren't lines of people at those bins. I figured my mother must be the most clever mother anywhere.

OTHER BOOKS YOU MAY ENJOY

One

FOR THE

Murphys

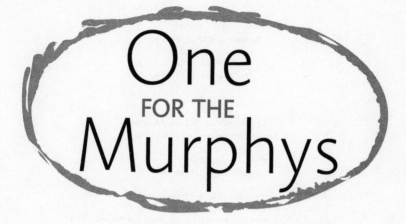

One
FOR THE
Murphys

Lynda Mullaly Hunt

PUFFIN BOOKS
An Imprint of Penguin Group (USA)

PUFFIN BOOKS
Published by the Penguin Group
Penguin Group (USA) LLC
375 Hudson Street
New York, New York 10014

USA • Canada • UK • Ireland • Australia
New Zealand • India • South Africa • China

penguin.com
A Penguin Random House Company

First published in the United States of America by Nancy Paulsen Books,
an imprint of Penguin Young Readers Group, 2012
Published by Puffin Books, an imprint of Penguin Young Readers Group, 2013

Copyright © 2012 by Lynda Mullaly Hunt

Penguin supports copyright. Copyright fuels creativity, encourages diverse voices,
promotes free speech, and creates a vibrant culture. Thank you for buying an authorized
edition of this book and for complying with copyright laws by not reproducing, scanning,
or distributing any part of it in any form without permission. You are supporting writers
and allowing Penguin to continue to publish books for every reader.

THE LIBRARY OF CONGRESS HAS CATALOGED THE NANCY PAULSEN BOOKS EDITION AS FOLLOWS:
Hunt, Lynda Mullaly.
One for the Murphys / Lynda Mullaly Hunt.
p. cm.
Summary: "After heartbreaking betrayal, Carley is sent to live with a foster family and struggles
with opening herself up to their love."—Provided by publisher.
ISBN 978-0-399-25615-8 (hc)
[1. Foster home care—Fiction. 2. Mothers and daughters—Fiction. 3. Stepfathers—Fiction.
4. Family problems—Fiction. 5. Family life—Connecticut—Fiction. 6. Connecticut—Fiction.]
I. Title. PZ7.H9159One 2012 [Fic]—dc23 2011046708

Puffin Books ISBN 978-0-14-242652-4

Printed in the United States of America

11 13 15 17 19 20 18 16 14 12

For Greg—My Hero

AND

For Judy—Maker of Miracles

CONTENTS

One
FOR THE
Murphys

CHAPTER 1

Lucky Girl

Sitting in the back of the social worker's car, I try to remember how my mother has always said to never show your fear. She'd be disappointed to see me now. Shaking. Just going without a fight.

The social worker, Mrs. MacAvoy, pulls out of the hospital parking lot while I play with the electric-lock button on her car door. *Lock. Unlock. Lock. Unlock.* She glares at me in the mirror and says, "Please . . . stop that. The door needs to stay locked."

I love it when people use the word *please* but they sound like they want to remove your face. I stop. But I'm not doing it to bug her like she thinks. It's just that I can't keep still. And it beats jumping out of a moving car.

My fingers play with my hospital bracelet. I stare at my name. Carley Connors. Thirteen letters. How unlucky can one person be?

I think about my mother. Still there, lying in her hospital bed like an eggplant. I wonder if she's conscious yet. I wonder why no one will tell me what's happening with her. And I wonder why I can't seem to ask anymore.

Gazing out the window, I count the trees. Connecticut is covered with them, but in March the branches are still bare. Like long, gray fingers waving us along as we speed by.

"We're almost there," Mrs. MacAvoy says, taking a corner faster than I think any social worker is supposed to.

I think back to sitting in that hospital bed, bunching the blankets up in my fists, asking her if they were going to send me to an orphanage. "We don't call them orphanages anymore," she'd said, shaking her head and laughing. Like *that* was the point?

Now I'm trapped in her car going to a place she's chosen. After what my stepfather has done, I'm terrified thinking about what kind of foster house I may land in. The things that could happen to me.

I think of the Little Mermaid mural near the nurse's station. How the tooth fairy gave me that CD when I was seven, and my mother let me get up to listen when I found it under my pillow at midnight. We danced around the kitchen together. She sang "Kiss the Girl" as she chased me to get a kiss. I never once ran away for real.

"You know," Mrs. MacAvoy says, pulling me back to reality. "You're very lucky, Carley."

"You're kidding me, right?"

Her mouth bunches up. "Well." She sounds like a ticking bomb. "It's a nice home. A good placement. You *are* lucky."

"Guess I should buy a lottery ticket then."

"Someday, Carley, you're going to have to realize that being angry at the whole world only hurts you."

I wonder if that isn't the point.

We drive up to a house the color of dirt. Tall, thin trees surround it, like guards on watch. There is a "66" on the mailbox. A palindrome.

Mrs. MacAvoy opens the car door for me. "This is a very nice family, *Carley*." She puts emphasis on my name as if to give me a warning. "And this is the first time they've taken a foster child . . ."

I know this is her way of telling me to be a "good girl." The walk up the driveway feels like wading through glue. I've read books and seen movies. I know what foster parents are like. They smoke cigars and feed you saltines for breakfast.

One, two, three . . . seven, eight, nine. Standing on the porch, I count the leaves on the plastic wreath that hangs on the door. The bright redness of the flowers reminds me of the swirling lights of the ambulance. I have a vague memory of my mother screaming for me and my own voice trying to yell for her. And the taste of blood; I remember that.

I remember the blinding pain surging through my body and then feeling nothing at all. Wondering if a person like me would go to heaven.

I jump when the door swings open, and a woman smiles. She is the kind of person you'd never look at twice. Her hair is shoulder length, straight, and different shades of brown. Her blue V-neck sweater matches her eyes, and she wears a silver leaf necklace and plaid pants. I mean, *plaid* pants?

She holds out her hand. "Hello, Carley. How nice to meet you. I'm Julie Murphy."

I can't reach back. Even the name feels fake. Too perky. I wonder why she's happy to meet me. I wonder how much she knows. And I hope that I do not like her.

Then this whole thing gets even worse.

Mrs. Murphy steps to the side. Behind her stand three boys. The smallest one runs over, stretching his hands up toward his mother, and she swoops him up.

I can't stay here. I'm probably here to be a live-in babysitter or a modern-day Cinderella.

The oldest boy looks at me like he wants to wrap me in a carpet and leave me on the curb.

I haven't cried since my mother told me she was going to marry Dennis. That was 384 days ago, but I want to cry now.

His mother tips her head to the side and holds my gaze until I just can't look anymore. I hear her voice. Soft. "Why don't you come in, Carley?"

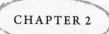

CHAPTER 2

The First Step

While Mrs. MacAvoy blathers on, Mrs. Murphy focuses on the bruises on my arms; her look of pity crawls inside of me. Clasping my hands behind my back, I try to hide my arms so she can't see.

The middle boy starts pulling Matchbox cars from his pants pockets and holds them against his chest. He's the dirtiest but seems the most serious, even with a head full of red curls.

The one in her arms is about four, I guess. He wears a plastic fireman's hat, little fire hydrant boxers, and bright yellow rain boots. A great blackmail picture when the kid's about sixteen.

"This is Daniel," she says, pointing to the tallest one. "And my redheaded car guy is Adam, and my littlest guy is Michael Eric. Say hi, guys!"

I look at this family. A family I don't know. That I am supposed to stay with. I try to swallow my panic.

The whole place smells like dryer sheets. Reminds me of Lucky's Laundromat back in Vegas, but it isn't nearly as bright. The fireplace spans an entire wall in the step-down family room; the mantel is covered with St. Patrick's Day decorations.

Mrs. MacAvoy leaves, saying, "Good luck." I wonder which one of us she's talking to.

When Mrs. Murphy closes the door behind her, she turns to me.

"Let's get you settled in," she says. The idea of me settling in here is about as likely as an apple tree sprouting in my ear.

She picks up the backpack that Family Services gave me, which has a stuffed giraffe, a toothbrush, and a pair of bright yellow fairy pajamas that remind me that there are worse things than death. The stuffed giraffe is good, though. Anyone who has had her whole life shredded in one night should have a stuffed giraffe.

Mrs. Murphy takes me up the staircase. There are thirteen steps to the top, the tenth one being a squeaker. Soon we stand in a bedroom decorated in the theme of fire trucks. On the wall over the bed, there's a red wooden sign that reads BE SOMEONE'S HERO in white letters, and I consider the cruel irony of sleeping under this phrase.

"Sorry about the room. I know it isn't well suited to a girl your age. I moved Michael Eric in with Adam so you'd have some privacy. You know, I assumed you'd be a boy." She looks at me over her shoulder and seems a little embarrassed. "I mean, I was surprised to hear that you were a girl."

"Yeah, me too."

Straightening the corner of the bed, she laughs. "What a clip."

I wonder what that means. I like it.

"I was thinking. If you want to call me Julie instead of Mrs. Murphy, that would be fine. Not so formal."

"Okay," I say, thinking that I don't want to call her Julie like we're friends. I don't want to call her anything. She seems okay, but I don't want someone else's family.

"I'm going to get Michael Eric and Adam cleaned up and start dinner. Mrs. MacAvoy said you'd been asking for books at the hospital, so I put a bunch you may like on the top shelf there." She nods toward a bookcase.

I turn to look at them. Best thing so far.

"We're having lasagna for dinner. I hope that's okay."

"Stouffer's or store brand?"

"Uh, no. I mean neither. I made it a couple of weeks ago and stuck it in the basement freezer." She seems embarrassed. "So I guess you could say it's frozen, then?"

She made it herself? Seriously?

Mrs. Murphy turns to go, closing the door behind her.

"Hey!"

"Yeah?" she answers, stepping back in.

"Do you have a husband?" I ask, staring at her wedding band and thinking of my stepfather, Dennis.

"Yes, I do." She sounds all singsongy. "My husband, Jack, is working at the firehouse today, but he'll be home tomorrow morning. He knows you're here."

I am afraid again. "Okay. Thanks."

She leaves, and soon I hear splashing from the bathroom and

it sounds like there are ten boys in the tub instead of two. I stand at the door and want to go in but don't. I see the Murphys' bedroom door is open, so I go in there instead.

The bed is high off the ground and has a woven canopy over it. There are pictures all over the room on tables and shelves. There's a man in a Navy uniform. There's also a wedding picture, and I see that the groom is the same as the Navy guy. I wish my mother had been married to my father.

The bathroom door opens behind me, and I feel like I've been caught doing something wrong. I jump back into the table, and the Navy man picture smashes on the floor. I blurt out, "Sorry."

"Carley. Never mind that. I'll clean it later. But be careful. Don't cut yourself."

I stare at her. When will she get mad?

"There's a little step stool in here," she says. "Why don't you come sit and join us?"

What sounds like a plastic cup falls on the floor in the bathroom followed by a loud little-boy laugh. She pokes her head in. "Michael Eric. Leave the water in the tub, honey."

Honey.

She turns toward me, waiting for an answer. I can see she becomes impatient as her gaze jumps between me and the bathroom.

"Sorry," I say. I wonder if my mother is awake yet.

She seems to force a smile. "The picture is no big deal. Jack hates it anyway."

My mouth dries up. I know I am not apologizing for the picture. I am sorry for being there in the first place.

Mrs. Murphy lets me skip dinner. Says it's only for the first night. I hear a happy family downstairs, talking and laughing, and I am relieved that I am not with them.

In the dark bedroom that is not my own, I count the wheels on the trucks over and over. I count the little firemen running around to help people. I stare at the hero sign and count the curves and lines of the letters. I wonder if, in my whole life, I could ever be someone's hero.

I think I hear my mother calling my name in the night, and I pull the covers up under my chin. I remind myself how she told me to never cry. How she and her friends would laugh at me when I did. How my mother would tell me that crying was for suckers, and that you can't be a sucker in Vegas.

I know that wherever my mother is, she has to be thinking about me, and I know I will go to her if she needs me, no matter what the state says. I hope that if I'm patient, I will have a mother of my own again.

CHAPTER 3

Orange You Glad You're Here?

A t night, the house is quiet. Too quiet for sleeping.

The digital clock reads 2:34 a.m.; I like the consecutive numbers. I watch and wait for 2:35 because two plus three will be five. At 2:36, two times three will be six.

The number six makes me remember my mother's favorite vase. How I filled it with six big, clear marbles with deep blue swirls inside, even when she told me not to. How my elbow sent it to the carpeted floor, and how when we cleaned it up, there were six pieces. We glued the vase back together, but it was misshapen and couldn't hold water anymore.

I'm afraid that's the way my mother and I will be now. I'm afraid that no matter how many times I apologize for messing things up with her new husband, Dennis, we will remain misshapen and unable to hold water.

I so wish I'd been able to see her before leaving the hospital. I think back to my last night there—just twenty-four hours ago. About how I tried to sneak out of my room and find my mother in intensive care. How I kept thinking that if I was any daughter at all, I'd be able to find her.

When the nurse caught me, I blurted out to her how sorry I was for making Dennis mad. Like by telling her, my mother would know too.

The nurse walked me back to my room and told me to get some sleep. I don't know why, when things are horrible, people always tell you to get some sleep. I bet it's because if you're asleep, they know you'll leave them alone.

When she turned to leave, I remember thinking that I was afraid to be alone.

The nurse turned out the lights before she left. And I was in the dark.

Just like I am now.

The next morning, I sip orange juice. Good, ordinary, boring orange juice with no added kiwi or pomegranate.

Mrs. Murphy went out last night to get it for me after I told her I only liked it plain. I think it's freakish that she got it just because I'd asked for it. Whenever I'd asked my mother for orange juice, she'd ask me if I were a Rockefeller. For years I'd thought that a Rockefeller was a person who really loves oranges.

The back door slams and there's instant screaming and crying; now this place finally feels a little like home.

Michael Eric comes in with his hand tucked into his armpit. His mother drops to the floor like someone has kicked her behind the knees, but she lands gently, holding out her arms, and he melts into them. He tells how Adam smashed his hand. She takes his hand and kisses it. "My poor ole boy," she whispers. "Does that feel better?"

His crying stops.

She wipes his tears away and he spins and runs back outside. Then Mrs. Murphy goes to the door and calls Adam.

Again she kneels and asks him if he hit his little brother. At first he denies it. Then she poses a simple question. "Are you telling me the truth?"

She's got to be kidding. If there's half a brain in his head, he'll stick to the story.

He pauses and says, "I whaled him, Mommy, but he deserved it."

I think that it's funny to have "whaled him" and "Mommy" in the same sentence, and I decide that I like Adam.

She tilts her head. "What have we said about this?"

"I'm supposed to protect him 'cause he's my brother."

"That's right. Brothers stick together, right? Family looks out for family."

I stand in a place with no space.

My stomach has such a longing in it that I want to throw up. The tone, the look on her face and the look on his, a gentle brush of his hair. A kiss on top of the head. I struggle to decipher a foreign language. She's looking at him like she's seeing the best thing ever. Even though he's done something wrong.

I no longer have the stomach for this juice that she bought for me. I go to the sink and pour it out. I don't belong here. I begin to think that a foster mother who smokes cigars and makes me sleep in the basement would be a relief.

CHAPTER 4

Are You There, God? It's Me, Carley

When Mrs. Murphy comes back into the kitchen, she looks nervous as she studies me. She seems to think about things a lot before she speaks, which makes me wonder what she doesn't say.

"So," Mrs. Murphy begins, in her perky voice. "Do you know what you'd like to do today?"

I shrug. What's with her? She makes it sound like I'm on a vacation.

"Would it be okay if I go shoot baskets?"

"You play basketball?" Perky Murphy asks.

"Yeah, I was on the team back home." I remember how my mother would come to the games and yell for me. How she'd tell the refs to go back to reffing blind man's basketball when they made a call against me. How I thought it was funny, but the other mothers used to tell her that it was inappropriate, which only made her louder.

"Well, you and Daniel should get along really well."

"*Great*," I say, thinking that I'll be back with my mother before that could even happen.

"You can borrow my coat," she says. "It's cold."

I can't because she suggested it.

She glances at me and then glances again. "You may borrow that, if you'd rather," she says, motioning toward a gray hoodie. I put it on.

Outside, I find a basketball right away. It's green with shamrocks. Can't *anything* just be the way I expect around here?

It's cold outside. Not like Vegas. I can see my breath, and it reminds me of the smoke in the casinos when my mother would leave me in the lobby to wait for her. She'd do a few of the slot machines just inside the door where she could see me waiting on the bench. How she'd do a thumbs-up when she won, or yell "Send me luck!" when she didn't.

Standing there in the cold, in front of the house that's the color of dirt, I decide to ask God a question.

I close my eyes and turn the ball in my hands. I say in a whisper, "Okay. If I make this basket, then my mother still loves me."

Bending my knees, I shoot, watching the ball spin in the air. It gets wedged between the board and the back of the hoop. I know that means something, but I don't know what.

"Wicked good one," says a voice behind me. At first, I think it's God. Like he has time to talk to me.

I turn around.

It's Daniel. "You going to get it down now?" he asks.

"What do you mean? I did the work of getting it up there; *you* get it down."

I hear a car. Daniel waves to a guy pulling into the driveway in a pickup. It must be Mr. Murphy.

Stellar. Just *stell*ar.

The door of the truck squeaks when he opens it. He slams the door, messes Daniel's hair, looks up at the ball, and says, "Good shot."

"It was *her*," Daniel says, pointing.

Mr. Murphy comes toward me, faster than I would like. He holds out his hand. "Nice to meet you, Carley," he says, but his face says that I'm here to infect his family with malaria. He makes me want to run.

Mrs. Murphy comes out through the garage. Mr. Murphy kisses her on the cheek and whispers something. She smiles at him. Then he grabs a small duffel bag from his truck and heads inside.

"Mom," Daniel says, pointing. "Look what she did."

Mrs. Murphy's smile falls away, and now she's rattled. I hear worry in her voice. "So get it down, Daniel. Problem solving, right?"

Clearly, he wanted a little of my blood instead of a suggestion to do it himself. I hardly know Daniel, but I hate him anyway. I have this feeling, though, that if I don't lay off the prince, Mrs. MacAvoy will be back for me.

CHAPTER 5

I Should Have Licked the Anthill

I came up to the fireman room after Daniel complained that I'm wearing his sweatshirt. I hate having to wear his clothes, but I'm glad the sleeves cover my bruises. No more pity face from his mother.

I sit on the floor, holding the giraffe that came in my Family Services backpack, rubbing my finger back and forth along its soft brown mane.

Michael Eric walks in.

"Don't you knock first?" I ask.

"But this is *my* room," he says.

Oh yeah.

He marches over and sits down. "Whatcha doin'?"

"Just thinking."

"Why would you be doing just that?"

17

I almost laugh at how little he knows of the world. "Sometimes you can't help but think, even if you don't want to."

"Like when you pee in your pants?"

I laugh now. Maybe he knows more than I thought. "Yeah. Kind of like that. Not so messy, though."

He giggles this laugh that comes right from his belly. If a sound could dance, this is what it would be like. He reaches for the giraffe, and I let him take it. He holds it against the side of his face. "Who is this?" he asks.

"Just a stuffed giraffe."

"Well, what's his *name*?"

"He doesn't have a name," I say.

He looks at the giraffe like he doesn't recognize it anymore. Then he hugs it to his stomach. "Mr. Longneck."

"Mr. Longneck, huh?"

"Yeah, 'cause he's got a long neck." He holds it in front of my face. "See?"

"Funny. I hadn't noticed that."

"Silly Carley. Of *course* a giraffe has a long neck. That's what makes him a giraffe!"

Funny how something can be defined by the one thing that makes it different from everything else. Like "the foster kid."

I turn to him and act confused. "I thought a giraffe had a trunk."

"No," he says like he feels sorry for me. He leans over and whispers in my ear. "That's an elephant."

"Oh. Well, thanks for setting me straight."

He sits up. "That's okay. I don't mind."

I have to smile. I like Michael Eric, too. How can he and Adam possibly be related to Daniel?

"Can I keep Mr. Longneck?" he asks me.

I'm surprised. I mean, I know I should give it to him because he's a little kid and everything, but besides the clothes I'm wearing and my high tops, Mr. Longneck is pretty much all I have in the whole world right now. "Sorry, bud. I don't think so."

He shrugs. "Oh," he says. Then his eyebrows jump. "Can you play with me?"

I feel like I should, but I really just want to sit. "Can we another time maybe?"

He stands and then bends over so his face is upside down. "We'll play on Friday. Oh, and Mommy wants you to come down for lunch now."

I'd rather lick an anthill than eat lunch, but I nod, and he is out as fast as he was in.

Perky Murphy stands near the sink making sandwiches. She turns to me. "Chicken, ham, or tuna?"

"I can make it myself."

"Don't be silly." She smiles. "Let me make it for you."

I don't *want* her to make it for me.

"So, which one do you think?" she asks.

"I really don't mind making it myself." I don't want her to wait on me. It feels wrong.

"I really don't mind, Carley. I mean, c'mon, it's only a sandwich. Chicken, ham, or tuna?" Her eyes widen.

19

I am dying to say roast beef.

"Perhaps you'd prefer something from the cabinet? There are some microwavable meals in there."

I almost feel sorry for her. She's so pathetic. Like the world would come apart if everyone doesn't get a perfect little lunch. I think of how watching my mother talk to her would be like watching a kitten play with a ball of yarn.

But the feeling in my gut whispers that maybe I'm a little mad about all the gallons of chicken noodle soup I've eaten right out of the can. Still though, this Perky Murphy is as fragile as they come.

She wouldn't last a second in my world.

I open the cabinet looking for a can of chicken noodle soup, so that I can feel like I'm in my own place. The first thing I notice are the Oreos. My mother's favorite.

I almost burst out laughing, though, when I see how everything is arranged by size with the labels facing forward. I mumble to myself, "And on the third day, God created the seas and the mountains and this freakish cabinet in Connecticut."

Yet looking at it, something creeps across my scalp. So while Mrs. Murphy is distracted by Michael Eric stuffing his entire sandwich in his mouth at once, I mess everything up, turning the cans around and upside down. The earth should fall off its axis when she opens this.

I sit down, holding a can of soup, trying to decide if I should eat it cold or not. Daniel shows up; he and his mom discuss what he should eat. Like the leaders of two nations have come together to work out something actually important. These people are too much.

The prince decides on cheese ravioli, so she goes to the cabinet. When she finds my redecorating, she lets out the longest sigh ever and says, "You know, Daniel, there is no need to leave things in such a mess. I try hard to . . ."

Could I possibly be this lucky?

"I didn't do it!" the little creep interrupts. And then they both stop and look at me, and I hold up a newspaper on the table to hide my laughter.

"Well, I guess we have a little prankster in our midst," Mrs. Murphy says.

"Oh that's great!" he yells. "I get in trouble, but if it's her you say"—he raises his tone to sound like a girl—"we have a little prankster in our midst."

"Daniel . . . ," she says.

"Just forget it!" he shouts and he's gone. A door slams, and it looks like it hurts her inside, and maybe I feel a little bad. Maybe.

Suddenly there is more crying, as Michael Eric bursts through the door. Why do these people cry so much?

"Mommy!" he yells. "Jimmy Partin hit me."

"Now, why would he do that?"

"For breathing, he said."

"He did, huh?" she says, squatting. She ruffles his hair. "You look okay, pal. Didn't I tell you to stay away from his yard?"

My mother used to call me *pal*. She even had a song about it. He nods.

"Well, Michael Eric, if you go *looking* for trouble, you're sure to *find* it."

I wish someone had told me that.

CHAPTER 6

Lettuce Pray

That night, Mrs. Murphy appears in my doorway.

"You know, Carley," she says, sitting on the bed, "it seems that you may be here awhile. We'll probably have to enroll you in school, don't you think?"

"I don't think it will be long. My mother will be out of the hospital soon."

She clears her throat. "Well, she will be okay, but it might take some time. A couple of months."

A. Couple. Of. Months. Those words took a long time to come out. Like she drew them as a line in the sky. I can't stay here a couple of months. There must be something in my face, because she tilts her head and asks, "Carley? Haven't you been in school since you've been in Connecticut?"

I think for a second to lie but decide there's no point. "My mother said that I would learn more about the real world by living life rather than sitting at a desk."

Worry is written on her face. "Well, I'll give you a few days to settle in, Carley, but I think it's important that you go to school." She pauses, then asks, "Why don't you come down and help me make dinner?"

"I'm not hungry."

"Now, I thought we agreed that you'd come to the table tonight."

I nod. And it turns out that "helping" with dinner is easy. She pours me a glass of milk while I sit on the counter. I am surprised to find she cares if I want a small or big glass and if I'd like a squirt of chocolate.

I swing my feet, but seeing her glance over at my foot hitting the cabinets stops me. I can't sit still, though. I try to come up with something to say that doesn't sound dumb, but I can't help thinking about my mother. Imagining her face and hearing her voice. Wondering if she's going to be okay.

Mrs. Murphy glances over at me. I know I should say something, but I worry about saying the wrong thing. I worry that I'll make her mad. I worry that I shouldn't have messed up her cabinet today. The only bright spot is that her husband is staying at the firehouse tonight.

"So . . . uh, Mr. Murphy is a fireman?"

"Yeah. And he's like a little boy about it. Loves it. That . . . and the Red Sox."

"Does he usually stay there overnight like this?"

"All the firefighters do. Actually, Jack's the captain, so sometimes it's a few days at a time."

I am relieved. "Does he get mad?" I blurt out.

"Why would you ask that?"

"I broke his picture upstairs. I was thinking he'd be mad."

She waves her hand in the air. "Honestly, Carley. Jack didn't even notice that the picture disappeared."

I bite down on the rim of the glass. "But does he get mad about things?"

"Jack? No." She puts down the knife. Then she takes a step and reaches toward me. I lean away quick.

"I'm sorry, Carley. I sense you like people to stay away from you."

My head wishes that, but the rest of me doesn't.

"Carley. Jack is a very good guy." She tries to make eye contact. "You're safe here."

She seems to believe I'm safe, but I don't know if I'll ever feel safe again.

Mrs. Murphy measures out water for some sauce on the stove. She adds a little, holds the measuring cup up to study it, pours a little out, studies it, adds a little, adds a little more, studies it, and finally pours it into the pan.

I guess a little extra water would be deadly for us all. We didn't even own measuring cups at home. My mother always said that one of those highball glasses from the casino was close enough to a cup.

"Do you want help?" I ask, pointing at the lettuce. I am nervous about doing it the way she wants, but I ask anyway.

"No, no. You relax. Just keep me company."

I can't believe that anyone would ask me to keep them company. She must be nuts.

"So," she begins. "You grew up in Las Vegas. That must be an exciting place to live, huh?"

"Not if you're a kid. Can't do anything, really."

"I see." She washes a tomato. "Well, I grew up in a town that couldn't be more different than Las Vegas."

I say nothing.

"So, then, I guess you just moved to Connecticut recently?" she asks me.

"Yeah."

"Do you like it?"

Is she *kidding* me? "Not so far."

She seems flustered. "I'm so sorry, Carley. That was dumb." She turns to me with such softness. "Do you need anything else? Are you comfortable?"

"I'm good." But what I'm really thinking is that I feel like a bird flapping its wings underwater. I've never had anyone wait on me like this or wonder if I need anything. I'd be more comfortable if she would just stop talking to me in that voice like it matters to her whether I'm happy or not.

Everything is ready, so she calls the boys for dinner and we all sit down at the table.

Mrs. Murphy begins, "Thank you, dear Lord, for these gifts which we're about to receive. We thank you for our family, friends, and for the safety of our loved ones."

I'm thinking that I can't thank Him for any of that stuff. And, besides that, I just asked God one simple question at the basketball hoop, and what does He do?

". . . We also thank you for bringing Carley into our home. We're happy that she's here."

"*I'm* not happy she's here," Daniel snaps.

His mom looks at him, and her head drops a little. "That's a horrible thing to say. Apologize."

"Well, you say we aren't supposed to lie, and *I* want her to go."

"Lying is wrong, but I don't think that God—or me, for that matter—wants you to hurt someone else's feelings. You can apologize or go to your room."

Daniel stands. "Fine."

"Daniel."

He disappears around the corner, and Mrs. Murphy's fork lands on her plate. "I'm sorry, Carley. I'll talk to him later on."

My body tingles the same way your foot does when it's asleep. I want to tell Daniel that I don't blame him, and that I'm trapped here with him just as he's trapped here with me. I have to admit, though, that I like thinking about how Mrs. Murphy talked to me earlier like there was no one else in the world.

Daniel reappears, and Mrs. Murphy looks up at him. I can see the relief in her face. "I'm glad you've come back. Are you ready to apologize?"

"How long is she staying, anyway?" he asks.

"I really don't know, Daniel. As long as she needs to."

I suddenly need to go.

"I want her to leave. She isn't in our family."

"Daniel." I sense panic in her voice. "We'll discuss this later."

"I don't want to."

"Why don't you sit down and eat something?"

"I don't want to."

Daniel glares, and I am surprised at how his words cut me. "Just because your mother doesn't want you doesn't mean you can take mine."

He runs.

And so do I.

CHAPTER 7

Upward and All Around

I run out through the garage and into the night. The blast of cold air shocks me. I scramble across the yard, looking back to see if Mrs. Murphy is at the door. She isn't there. Of course. Why would someone else's mother care about me?

I sprint up the hill and around the curve of the road, picking up more speed. Every time my socks hit the concrete, pebbles and sticks shoot pain through my feet. But I won't allow myself to slow down. "Go, Carley," I say through clenched teeth. "Run. Run away."

My fingernails dig into my palms. Every time I inhale, my chest aches. But with every pain, every sting, every ache . . . I only run faster.

Every time my right foot touches the ground, I say, "No."

No to crying.

No to the Murphys.

No to me.

My body wants to slow down, but I force my legs to move. To speed up while my "No" becomes one long, continuous word—a pleading. A prayer to please make things different.

And just as the pain makes my chest feel like it will explode, there's no pain at all. Just a blur of things. Cold wind. An orchard. The sound of dried leaves tumbling across the ground. My parched mouth.

I fall. Slowly.

My palms and face rest on the dirt before I fall to my side, curled up like a caterpillar that's been touched.

I think about my own mother. Could it be that she really doesn't want me anymore? Is she mad about how I messed with Dennis? Made him so mad.

My mind plays a movie for me. The movie of the night everything tipped upward and all around.

I had been dribbling my basketball. The faded one with no bumps left from constant use.

My mother smelled like vodka when she came in, complaining about me bouncing the ball inside. I wasn't too surprised when she lunged for it. I jumped to the side and she stumbled, then landed on the floor. She held her leg, her face twisted in pain. "Carley," she yelled. "You better show me some respect!"

Her new husband, Dennis, who had been fired as an Elvis

impersonator back in Vegas, came in wearing his paste-on black side-burns to check on his howling wife.

He asked me what I'd done and I said, "All I did was move out of her way."

Einstein spoke. "That don't explain why she's laying on the floor."

"Why? Are you the only one who can hit her?" This wasn't smart to say, but the bruises I had seen on my mother—even before their wedding—made me so mad.

"What I done to her is nothing compared to what I'm gonna do to you," he said.

My mother watched, groaning as she held her leg.

I ran around the dining room table as he tried to catch me, steadying himself on the table as he went.

"Hey, Dennis. How does one get fired as an Elvis impersonator? Is it because you sing like your foot is caught in a steel trap?" Another dumb thing to say, but I'd decided to egg him on, to really annoy him. Because I had just come up with a master plan to show my mother why she had to leave him.

He lunged at me across the top of the table and I jumped back. If it weren't for his fat stomach, he might have gotten me.

"I hate you, Dennis. You're nothing but a loser."

He slammed his fist on the table, but his voice was quiet and intense. "Too bad I'll be the last thing you ever see."

My plan suddenly felt like a suicide mission, but I knew that if he hit me, my mother would be angry. One good belt is all I would have to take, and she would tell him to go. Forever.

I was ready.

I held up an imaginary microphone, and I sang "Don't Be Cruel."

"I'm gonna shut you up for good, little girl."

My mother cried out for me, and I moved toward her.

Something clamped around my ankle. I looked down and it was my mother's hand holding me. She needed my help.

"Mom! What's wrong? Is it your leg?"

But she didn't answer. Instead she spoke to Dennis. "Honey, I got her! I got her by the foot!"

CHAPTER 8

Wake Up and Smell the Apple Juice

My face itches. My eyelids flutter. I smell apple juice.

I open my eyes expecting to see a nurse, but instead I see tree branches and a black-velvet sky sprinkled with silver glitter. I am freezing and wonder if I'm finally dead.

I hear my name.

Turning my head, I see Mrs. Murphy and I am confused.

I can still feel my mother's hand on my ankle and the first hit from Dennis. Harder than I imagined it could be. And then I think how I couldn't remember anything that happened after that or how my mother landed in the hospital too.

"Carley?" Mrs. Murphy whispers.

My first question surprises me. "Where are the boys?" I mumble.

"They're fine. I called Jack and asked him to come home."

I think that she belongs with them and not with me and if she left me in this orchard forever, I would be happy. I could be the wild girl raised by the apple trees. This would be my excuse for not fitting into society.

"It's so cold, Carley. Let's get you home." She reaches for me.

Home? I don't have a home. And I can't believe this woman I don't even know is reaching for me. I never cry anymore, but with this woman's open hand in front of me and the memory of my mother's hands around my ankle, I almost lose it.

It hurts, but I let her pull me up. I stare at my feet as we walk back to the house. Wondering why she cares what happens to me. Relieved we don't have to talk.

"Let's get you inside and warm," she says, opening the front door and stepping inside.

I follow. She closes the door and turns off a bunch of lights that were on outside.

"You have a lot of lights," I say.

"I had them all on because I was hoping you'd come back." Her smile is sad, like she'd worried as she turned on those lights.

"Why did you take me in, anyway?" I ask, unable to stand still and suddenly needing an answer.

"Well . . ." She sighs and puts her hands in her pockets. "I grew up with a friend in foster care. She really had a tough time, and I've never been able to shake her stories . . . And when I grew up, I wanted to help kids. That's how I ended up in teaching." She bites her lip. "Jack and I talked about taking in a needy child before, but we thought we'd wait until our own were much bigger."

Needy child. I don't like either word.

"But it had been on my mind, so I dropped by the foster care office just to get some information. I was curious about the kinds of kids there are."

Kinds of kids? Sounds like she's shopping for dishes.

"Well, I was sitting there in the office with this huge binder of children—so many of them, Carley . . ."

She heads into the kitchen, and I follow her.

". . . and feeling like I should do something. And then Mrs. MacAvoy comes in spitting nails about a kid she'd just met at the hospital. I could hear only some of what she said, but what I overheard was . . . well . . . pretty funny, actually."

I half smile.

"The thing is, she kept referring to you as 'Connors,' and so I assumed you were a boy. But there was just something. Some vibe. I wanted to help a kid with . . . personality, you know? A kid with some fight in them."

"So I can hit somebody?" I say, sitting in a chair. "Because, to tell you the truth, I would really like to hit somebody."

She takes a deep breath. "I understand, Carley, but no, you can't. But I don't blame you for feeling that way. I meant *fight* as in determination." She looks at me in a suspicious kind of way. "But I have a feeling you knew that."

I look up at her. "Sometimes you *need* to fight, you know. Even if you don't want to."

She nods slowly and says, "I understand."

But somehow I just don't see her as someone who knows real fighting. Fighting for her probably means getting the last sirloin steak at the grocery store.

"Can I get you something to eat? Are you thirsty?" she asks.

I realize that the last four letters in "Julie" are "u lie."

I stand, feeling like I suddenly have to give back all the nice things she's done. "Do you want your coat back?"

She shakes her head. Seems confused. I take off her coat and hand it to her even though she'd let me keep it. She offers to make me hot chocolate, which I want but can't seem to say yes to. She tries to be nice, making conversation, but it makes me distrust her all the more. It just doesn't make any sense to me as to why she would care whether I live or die.

After all . . .

My own mother doesn't.

What a Clip

Officially, this is my fourth day in captivity. I have started keeping the tally on the back of that dumb hero sign. One good thing, though. Mrs. Murphy has cleared some time to take me clothes shopping. In an actual store.

This is a far cry from my mother and I making late-night visits to Salvation Army drop boxes to "shop." I remember how she'd hand me a flashlight, hoist me into the bins, and then make requests for sizes and specific colors like I was sitting in there with a doting saleslady and a catalog.

It was cool, though, how we'd go to McDonald's afterward and my mother would hold up her ice cream as if to toast me. "Carley, what would I ever do without you?" she'd ask.

Back when I was little, I used to wonder why there weren't lines of people at those bins. I figured my mother must be the most clever mother anywhere.

. . .

We get into her car. I feel out of place without fast-food containers to kick out of the way. I am also feeling trapped, being strapped into a seat which puts me eight inches from Mrs. Murphy's elbow.

"So, what makes Carley Connors unique?" she asks.

I slide my hands under my thighs.

"C'mon, kid. Cough up the goods. Something about *you*."

She tugs at my insides, and I hate it. "Nothing to tell, really. I was born with two heads, so one was removed by surgeons. Unfortunately, they took the wrong one."

"Maybe you should have kept it. You'd have made a great referee."

She laughs, and I figure I'd rather have her laugh at my jokes than have to tell her anything real. I take a breath. "I'm captain of the Hawaiian downhill skiing team. Oh . . . I'm also perfecting my recipe for toast."

She laughs again, and then I hear her add something as if she's talking to herself and not to me. "What a clip."

I still like this. I wonder if it has anything to do with guns— the clip that holds the bullets. I would want to be that part.

"You're a real hot ticket, aren't you? Now tell me something real about yourself."

"So, what do you know about me already?"

"I know that you're pretty sharp."

Sharp as a marble.

"And I know that you're a nice girl." She looks over.

"Nice girl" is about the worst thing you can say about a

person. It says that there's nothing remarkable. It says that you make no impression whatsoever. My mother has always taught me to make an impression.

"I guess that means you don't know a thing about me."

She looks as if she knows the punch line of a joke that no one else does.

I say, "I'm in foster care. Doesn't that pretty much spell it out?"

She doesn't look at me but lets out a small laugh. "Hardly."

The mall is enormous. We quickly join the beehive of people. She picks up a shirt that says ANGEL on it; I just about swallow my tongue at the idea of wearing it.

"Oh. Isn't this cute?" She picks up a different shirt. A striped pink shirt with a white collar and three buttons. She holds it up in front of me. Like I'm ready for a day of golf at the country club.

I back away.

She tilts her head. "It would look wicked good on you, Carley!"

"Wicked good?" I laugh.

"Yeah, *wicked* good. You're in Red Sox Nation now. Well . . . close to it, anyway." She holds the shirt up again. "So? What do you think?"

I usually have no trouble expressing my opinions, but I'm usually with someone who lives on the same planet as me. And I worry. I worry about making her mad. I think of my mother and wonder what she would think of me wearing these clothes.

But living with my mother has also made me a good reader of people; I was trained to see things coming before they actually do. On the streets of Vegas, I learned how to figure people out—who really wanted directions to a casino and who wanted something else.

Mrs. Murphy's bent eyebrows and her slightly open, crooked mouth tell me that she wants to do this for me, and I know that, although she's a flake, I could do a lot worse.

I go into the dressing room and am relieved when she doesn't follow. I get dressed and look in the mirror. I feel like I'm wearing a Halloween costume. I also notice that my bruises are fading a little.

I come out, and Mrs. Murphy smiles and asks, "Do you like it?"

I don't know what to say.

"Do you like it, Carley? Are you happy with it?"

I can see that she really needs to hear that I do. Lying when I've had to hasn't been a problem for me before, so I wonder why I can stay quiet, but I can't make myself tell her that I like it.

CHAPTER 10

A Genie, Fresh Rolls, and a Penguin

We buy two bags of clothes and go to a restaurant.

"So, Carley, did you have fun shopping?"

"Thanks. I mean thank you for all the stuff you got me." I feel really guilty about the money she spent.

She looks up. "You're very welcome, Carley. Happy to do it."

I know I should be grateful, but I look at her and she suddenly makes me mad. Why does she pretend that we have some . . . I don't know . . . some *relationship*. My face must give me away, because she has that pity look again.

"Carley, is there anything wrong?"

I want my own mother. I feel like if she could see this she would be completely wrecked. I decide I hate all of those new clothes.

"You seem upset all of a sudden."

She scares me. I've been beaten and abandoned. I've been

chased by security guards and managers at casinos. Approached by creeps on the strip in Vegas. But no one scares me like this Mrs. Murphy. I feel like she can see the things I keep hidden. I feel like I can't protect myself from her.

"Look," I say. "Stop playing psychologist with me, okay? Maybe I don't want to talk."

"Carley, I'm sorry. Did I do something?"

"You know, maybe it's not about you . . . ," I say. She looks hurt, and I'm happy the pity look is gone. "Maybe I just don't want to talk to you. Why don't you . . . go home and iron something?"

Her back straightens. "You have no right to speak to me that way."

"I only told you to iron something. It's probably your favorite thing to do, right?" I hate myself.

A busboy, who looks pretty young to be working here, comes by wearing an apron. He places a basket of rolls on the table. "Can I start you off with water?"

I turn to him. "No, but can you bring me my mother?"

He opens his mouth, but no sound comes out.

Mrs. Murphy saves him. "I'm sorry. We'll need just another minute."

I look at the kid. "Do you have unlimited rolls here?"

"Uh-huh."

"Good," I say as I grab the basket of rolls and, one by one, stuff them down the side of the booth, wedging them between the cushion and the wall.

"What are you doing?" Mrs. Murphy asks.

"These aren't warm enough. I want more." I want to see her reaction, see her go berserk.

I read the kid's name tag. I say, "Rainer? *That's* your name? Do you have a brother named Thunder?"

He looks at me like I'm a jerk. He's probably right. When our waiter comes over to join him, Mrs. Murphy glares. "Carley, do you know what you want?"

My stomach screws into a knot. "I told you . . . what I want."

She smooths out the napkin already on her lap. "Well, how about something on the menu?" Mrs. Murphy's eyes bore through me.

I can't look at her, so I look over at Rainer. I can say what I want to him without consequences. Things I want to say to her but can't. "Do you have parents on the menu?"

"What are you talking about?" he asks, annoyed.

"I want my own mother back. What's so hard to understand?" My body is electric.

"Do you want to order or not?" the waiter asks, also annoyed.

"Did you know that 'tips' spelled backwards is 'spit'? You know, if you bring me a bowl . . ."

"Carley," Mrs. Murphy says. "Can we please just end this? What do you want to eat?"

I lean forward and stare her in the eye. "Bread and water. Like in prison."

Her long drawn-out sigh screams disapproval.

"I'm so very sorry," Mrs. Murphy says. "We'll just have two grilled chicken sandwiches and two orders of fries." The waiter scribbles it down and they both leave.

I have to give Perky Murphy credit for ordering. I figured she would have left with her coat over her head by now. What will it take to get her to just give up? I call to Rainer, who, unbelievably, turns around to look at me. "Oh, Rainer . . . Don't forget the rolls, will you." I wink.

"Carley," Mrs. Murphy says, and she reaches across the table to me. I study her hand. Freckles. Neat fingernails. Why does she think that I will touch her? What planet has she beamed down from? I mean, reach out to *her*? I'd sooner kick a beehive.

"I want to help you."

Liar.

I look at her. "Why don't you just send me back?"

"Is that what you want?"

I feel like if I move, I'm going to totally lose it. Like it would start as a little stream and end up as a raging river. So I don't move. The sandwiches come. I don't move. She takes two bites. I don't move. She asks the waiter for a box, pays the check, and stands, telling me it's time to go.

She reaches for me. And I jump.

"I'm sorry, Carley." She sighs and steps back. "Why don't we get going?"

She's apologizing to me?

I follow her out. Rainer waves like a doofus, and I blow him a kiss. Mrs. Murphy shakes her head but lets it go.

We get into the car. "Are you okay, Carley?"

"I'm fine." I watch a movie of myself running.

Running and running and running.

"I don't think you're okay," she replies.

"I told you not to play psychologist with me." I count things on the dashboard.

"It's okay to cry, Carley. You have good reasons. I can see you're filled right up to the top with it."

How can she see that? "I . . . *never* cry. What's the point? It's just weak."

"I know things are hard for you, but I think the release would make you feel better. You know, like shaking a Coke bottle. The pressure builds up."

"Don't play science professor with me either," I tell her.

"People are meant to cry," she says. "It's human nature and it might do you some good."

"What about penguins?"

"I don't think penguins cry."

I want to laugh at her. "No, but they have wings."

"You've lost me."

"Yeah. Look, penguins have wings but they don't fly. Nobody gets ticked at them. Hey . . ." I look her in the eye. "Why don't we go down to Antarctica and shove some poor unsuspecting penguin into a cannon. Tell him that because nature gave him wings, he's meant to fly. We'll launch the sucker, and when he lands in a broken, mangled heap . . . we'll ask Mr. Penguin if he's better off. If it's done him some good. What do ya say?" I pump two fists. "Are ya *with* me?"

She starts the car.

CHAPTER 11

High Tops Girl from the Planet Oblivion

After getting back from shopping, Mrs. Murphy does not argue when I tell her I'm going to bed. I crawl under the cold covers and think of the warmth of Vegas. How the sky is never dark, even at night. How I used to live there with my mother, and it was my home. How I only have one full day left before I have to go to school.

The next day is Sunday, and I spend most of it with my nose in a book entitled *Samurai Shortstop*. It's Daniel's and it's about baseball, but the twerp refuses to read it. It's actually pretty good.

Jack Murphy comes home after lunch. He does not say hello to me even though I'm standing right there when he comes in. Mrs. Murphy's face screws into worry. She puts her dish towel down and follows him upstairs. I figure this is more interesting than TV.

I stand at the bottom of the stairs and hear the deep sandpapery voice of Mr. Murphy—even rougher than usual.

"Julie. I *told* you this would be a mistake."

"We don't know that, Jack. We hardly know her at this point."

Oh my God. They're fighting about me?

"So are you going to tell me what happened last night?" he asks. "You came to bed crying and wouldn't tell me why. I know she did something."

I made her cry?

"And then . . . then," he continues, "I open the checkbook this morning to pay the bills, and I see you've spent a fortune on her. What were you thinking, Julie?"

She fires back. "It's important for a girl that age to have the right clothes. I'm sorry, but I thought it was worth it. I won't spend like that again. Besides, it's not *all* out of pocket, Jack. The state gives us money."

"Not enough for this. Let's look at what's happened so far. She fought with Daniel . . ."

"She didn't fight with him. *He* got upset."

"Well, you cannot call me at the station to come home because of drama with this girl."

Mrs. Murphy mumbles something I can't make out.

Then I hear her coming. I scurry back through the living room, through the back hallway, and into the family room. When she comes back into the kitchen, I am lounging on the couch, but my heart bangs like a drum.

My stomach aches. I feel guilty about the restaurant and I'd like to tell her how sorry I am, but I'm afraid if I stick my hand out, it'll be lopped off. No doubt that Jack Murphy would happily sharpen the ax for the job.

The younger boys come in from outside. Michael Eric walks over and leans in. "Carley Connors?"

I am surprised he speaks to me. Poor kid doesn't know any better. "Michael Eric Murphy?"

His eyes get big and he smiles like I've said "Abracadabra!"

Michael Eric pats me on the head. "Do you play? I mean, *ever* do you?"

"Play what?"

"Games and just other stuff."

Mrs. Murphy is at the sink, listening. I have a feeling that I can't really say no this time. I suppose I owe her.

I ask him, "What kinds of games do you like?"

He jumps into the air and comes down with his feet far apart and his fists up. "Superheroes!" He kicks the air and growls, which is funny because he thinks he's actually scary.

"Which superhero is your favorite?"

"Super Poopy Man!" He laughs hysterically.

"And I'm Butt Man!" Adam yells, jumping up on the love seat. His flaming red hair bounces with him. "Butt Man farts so bad, he flies!" Then Adam runs in a circle making fart sounds.

"Boys," Mrs. Murphy says, coming to the edge of the carpet. "That's enough. Let's not spiral into oblivion here."

"Where's oblivion, Mom?" calls Michael Eric.

"Does Super Poopy Man come from the planet Oblivion?" asks Adam.

Mrs. Murphy glances at me. "I will never understand their love of bathroom humor."

I get an idea. "Hey, guys, let's play a different superhero game.

I can be the bad guy." I lean over and look into Michael Eric's shimmering eyes. "And you can try to catch me."

The boys jump around like they're in the end zone of the big game. I jump up. "First, superheroes need capes!"

"Yeah!" Michael Eric yells.

Mrs. Murphy makes eye contact with me for the first time since the mall. She looks happy that I'm there, and I'd rather see her looking like this than the way she looked at the restaurant. I guess I don't want her to think helping me is a mistake.

But I can't believe I made her cry.

I lead the boys upstairs and take some towels out of the closet. I find a sewing kit in the closet and grab some safety pins. "Okay. Time to make capes!"

Adam stares at the pins and looks unhappy. "Real superheroes don't wear safety pins."

I want to tell him they don't wear towels either, but instead I find some towels that are big enough to knot. I laugh to myself about the terror a villain would feel in seeing someone coming after him wearing a Thomas the Tank Engine cape.

"I'm going to be Super Poopy Man again!" Michael Eric proclaims.

"What's *my* superhero name?" Adam asks.

His red hair is the first thing I think about. "How about Flame Thrower?"

He smiles. Then he frowns. "Daddy wouldn't like that one, I don't think."

"Oh yeah. Well . . . how about Red Sox Man? He hits home runs every time."

"Can I also have a wicked fast car and a freeze ray gun?"

"Sure!"

His big smile shows off his missing teeth.

I grab the first thing I see—a big rubber beetle—and proclaim, "I am"—I look down at my shoes—"I am Super High Tops Girl! I've captured the magic bug. With a power such as this, soon I will rule the world!" I end with crazy maniacal laughter, stick the bug under my arm, and rush past them.

Adam yells, "Get her! She must not escape! We must get the magic bug or the world will meet its doom!" Clearly, they've seen a lot of cartoons. Michael Eric echoes whatever his brother says by repeating his last two words and then yelling, "Yeah!"

"You'll never conquer me, for I am the most powerful Super High Tops Girl! I will destroy you with the toxic smell of my shoes!"

Adam jumps toward me and points his finger like a gun. "I'll shoot you with my freeze ray!"

"Freeze ray, yeah!" Michael Eric jumps.

Daniel watches.

I throw up my arms. "No, no! I'll block you with my heat gun and turn your freeze ray to *steam*!"

"Aw, cool," Adam mumbles.

We chase each other around until it's dinnertime. Before bedtime, Michael Eric comes over while I sit on the couch and kisses me good night on the knee.

Mr. Murphy seems surprised. His gaze lingers longer than is comfortable. "I guess you've won him over, huh?" he asks.

I shrug. "I guess."

Soon enough, I go up to bed. I worry about school the next day, but decide I'd better just set my thoughts on playing Super High Tops Girl and how much fun I had. Or how Mrs. Murphy smiled more at dinner than she has in a couple of days. I wonder how I had planned to be a bad guy but ended up with a hero's name.

From the planet Oblivion.

CHAPTER 12

Thou Art a Wing Nut

It is my sixth day here. My first day of school.

Mrs. Murphy, the boys, and I all pile into the car. I hold the lunch that Mrs. Murphy made for me, relieved that there are no smiley faces drawn on the bag. The boys are making up disgusting ice cream flavors as we pull into the Smith Middle School driveway. I wonder if the feeling in my stomach is from the thought of ant juice and broccoli ice cream or starting school.

I look up. Way nicer than my old school. Pillars the size of cars. Huge lawn with a row of perfect trees. All the same size. No leaves.

Mrs. Murphy turns to me. "The office is right inside the front door. Would you like me to walk you in?"

I'd kind of like her to, but I glance into the backseat and imagine two boys running in circles around us, and decide I'd rather be more invisible than that. "No, thanks."

As I get out, Michael Eric yells, "Bye-bye, Carley. See you after school!"

The wind whips as I walk, staring at my reflection, toward the glass doors of the school; I am unfamiliar to myself in my new clothes. I head into the office. "Hi. I'm a new student here? Eighth grade?"

I give the secretary my name; it's kind of nice talking to a secretary who doesn't know who my mother is. She shuffles some papers and smiles. "Looks like you're all set, Carley! Welcome to Smith!"

I am not breathing funny anymore by the time I find that the combination to my locker works. I close my eyes and take a deep breath. Maybe this will be okay.

"You're kidding me!" the girl next to me yells, hitting her locker. "What a simp I am. I can't believe I left it at home." She leans her forehead against her locker, straightens, and then turns to me. "Can you believe what a simp I am?"

She takes off a very cool black jacket with scenes from New York embroidered on it. Her shirt reads WICKED and has a small green witch on a broom.

"Well?" she asks.

"Well what?"

"Can you believe what a simp I am?"

This is a test, but I don't know what to say. I'm not standing in my own skin.

She leans in. "You don't know what *simp* means, do you?"

I lean back.

"As in *simpleton*?" she asks. "Or is that too long of a word for you?" She laughs. Her eyes get smaller and stare until I look away first. She swears and says, "What do you pathetic clones know, anyway?"

"What are you even talking about?"

She shifts her weight and then motions toward me. "Nice getup. Why, you're a real trailblazer."

I've always been fast on my feet in situations like this, but I just stand there. I look down at myself. I've wondered all morning if I'd be accepted more because of these popular clothes.

She slams her locker door and storms away, ranting about whatever it was she'd forgotten.

My breathing is funny again.

First period is social studies. I walk in and the teacher smiles at me. "Welcome. I'm Mr. Ruben. You know, like the sandwich?" He covers his stomach with one hand and waves the other in the air. "However, thou may address me as Sir Ruben." He takes a deep bow and I notice he's wearing orange Converse high tops. "You must be Maiden Carley Connors?"

"Uh-huh." Talk about a screw loose. He must be the original wing nut.

"Why don't thou takest a seat?"

I want to ask where I should *takest* it, but I see there is only one empty desk.

Unfortunately the seat is right next to the girl I met at the lockers. Talk about unlucky.

She rolls her eyes. "You have *got* to be kidding me," she mumbles.

Then I look to my left and it gets worse.

I recognize him immediately, but he isn't looking at me. He turns and then bam! He remembers. The guy from the restaurant the other night. Rainer. The guy I not only gave a hard time to, but also made it personal. He's chewing gum slowly as he stares me down. "Well, what do you know. It's our little orphan, Oliver Twist. Want some more rolls?"

The girl on my right looks at him like he's contagious. "Shut up, Rainer."

For some reason he backs down.

"Quiet down, ye villainous milk-livered minnows!" Sir Ruben's voice is deep. Mr. Ruben goes from student to student to see if everyone has their assignments; everyone does until he gets to the girl next to me. He asks, "And you, Princess Toni?"

"I've no interest in being the princess. I'll be the queen, if you don't mind."

Mr. Ruben smiles out of one side of his mouth. "Well, that will depend on whether thou art holding thee project!"

"Nope. Don't got it." She slumps back in her chair and folds her arms.

"Alas, Peasant Toni!" Mr. Ruben swings his pointer as he makes his way up the aisle. "Why in the world do thou want to give me a lumpish day?"

"Everyone needs a hobby" is her flat response and the class laughs again. I feel better to know she treats other people like that.

He turns and strolls back toward the front of the class. "Alas, Miss Toni Byars. You can always make me laugh. For this, I will let you live, pardon you even, and give you another generous and magnificent day to follow through on that most important assignment of yours." He turns to look at her. "Minus ten points, of course."

"Thank you, your *worship*."

When a long-haired kid says he hasn't finished, Mr. Ruben's eyebrows dance and he slaps the kid's desk with his pointer, exclaiming, "To the dungeon, ye pigeon egg!"

I quickly gather that he's a medieval history freak, his screws aren't loose but missing altogether, and he thinks that he's fourteen. Still, though, I like him.

CHAPTER 13

You Have the Right
to Remain Silent

So, tell me how your first day was." Mrs. Murphy sits at the kitchen counter and seems like she has nothing to do but listen to my answer. She is so odd. But it is nice. I remember how my mother never stopped talking long enough to listen to me. How I figured out that *silent* and *listen* are made of the same letters.

"Nothing too eventful. Social studies teacher is . . . uh . . . unique to say the least."

"How about the kids? Did you meet anyone?"

"Well, I learned a valuable lesson about karma."

"How do you mean?" she asks, leaning forward slightly.

I can't tell her about Rainer; she'd probably shatter. "Nothing. Just kidding."

"Well, I have no doubt you'll make friends before you know it."

"You know, there's only one letter difference between *friends* and *fiends*." Then I look up to see that she has a dopey smile. I mean, she's nice and everything, but give me a break.

The doorbell rings. "I'll get it," I say. Wow. Actually saved by the bell.

I swing the front door open and find a police officer.

Mrs. Murphy comes from the kitchen. She stops suddenly when she sees him and holds her breath.

The officer looks past me at her. "Hello, ma'am. Are you Julie Murphy?"

Mrs. Murphy puts her hand to her mouth. "Oh God. Is this about my husband?"

"Ma'am?"

"My husband, Jack Murphy. He's a Glastonbury firefighter. Is he hurt?"

The officer holds his hand up like he's directing traffic and shakes his head. "No. No, ma'am. I'm sure he's fine." He softens a bit. "I'm actually here about a foster care child you have. A Carley Connors?"

Mrs. Murphy's shoulders droop as she looks over at me.

The officer's name tag shows that his name has thirteen letters. How unlucky for him.

I hear the clamor of four feet running in our direction. Adam says, "I'm tellin' ya I saw a police car in the driveway!"

"Aw, wicked cool!" Adam says when he sees the officer.

"Hey there, little man."

Michael Eric steps up. "Do you shoot people a lot?"

"Of course he shoots people, dummy," answers Adam. "Why else would he have a gun?"

Mrs. Murphy puts her hand on Adam's shoulder. "I'm so sorry, Officer."

Michael Eric speaks again. "My daddy says policemen are brave."

"Well, you thank your daddy for me."

"My daddy's a firefighter," Adam says. The boys stand taller. "He's brave too."

"He must be." The officer nods.

Mrs. Murphy holds up her pointer finger. "Would you wait just a minute? I'm going to get them busy." She disappears with the boys. I look at the officer and decide to say nothing. I must be in trouble.

She returns quickly. "Nothing like television and lollipops in a pinch."

"Yes, ma'am."

"I'm sorry, Officer. Now, what can we do for you?"

"Would it be all right if I asked Carley a few questions?"

She steps back and waves him into the living room. Waves in someone who probably wants to drag me away in handcuffs. Nice.

I fold my arms. "I know my rights. I don't have to answer anything." I've heard people say that on television a million times. Half the battle in these things is letting them know you're not afraid.

"Look, miss. You're not in any trouble." He flips through the pages of his pad. "I am investigating an incident involving a Dennis Gray."

I freeze. I remember telling my mother his name spelled backwards was "sinned" and she laughed at me. Back when she first brought him home and I had a sick feeling about him.

He leans forward slightly. "You know him?"

I nod as my insides fold over and over.

"He's your stepfather, correct?"

"Unfortunately."

"Okay." His feet move farther apart. "So I guess you don't like him much?"

"No. Not much."

"Well, there are some things we need to clear up about the night you ended up in the hospital. Do you remember that night?"

"Not really." I only remember the beginning. Besides, I don't believe that I'm in no trouble at all.

"Now, Mr. Gray is under arrest for two counts of assault and battery, resisting arrest, and assaulting a police officer, among other things. He had quite a night for himself."

I feel like I'm going to throw up.

"The prosecutor was looking at two counts of attempted murder, but it's hard to prove intent to kill without hard evidence."

He was trying to *kill* me? And my mother too?

"We've been questioning him along this line. But Mr. Gray claims that your mother . . . well . . . that she helped him in the beating. So the prosecutor is considering charging your mother as well."

I look at Mrs. Murphy and stand straight. I say, "You don't have to stay if you don't want to."

She sits down and leans forward with her elbows on her knees. She bites the inside of her cheek and I can see she's trying hard not to cry.

"His report of the incident is that she held you down while he kicked your abdomen, chest, and back."

I remember. I remember how she did that. I've been trying to tell myself that I must have remembered it wrong, but here he is to tell me that my mind wasn't fooling me. I didn't think anything could hurt more than that beating.

I was wrong.

I don't want Mrs. Murphy to hear anything else, so I say again, "You don't have to stay."

She clears her throat and brushes her cheek with the back of her hand. "No. It's okay. I want to be here for you."

"I don't need you here. It's okay."

She takes a deep breath and stands. I look away.

"Carley." She says my name like it's a command. "There isn't anything . . . *anything* . . . that he can say that's going to change how I feel about you."

I think two things: One, I want to die, and two, how *does* she feel about me?

She leaves, and I miss her.

"So, Carley," the officer says, "is there any truth to that? Did your mother contribute in any way to your situation that night?"

Situation? Good word. "What did my mother say?"

"Your mother is heavily sedated. She will remain so for quite some time."

Great. So I have to decide. If I tell, will my mother end up in prison? She'd never forgive me for that. Would the Murphys keep me, or would I bounce around foster care like the kids in those TV movies? I don't seem to have a choice.

"I can't believe that you would believe a jerk like Dennis about anything. My mother would . . ." The rest of the sentence sticks in my throat. "My mother would never . . . hurt me." I force myself to look at him.

He nods slightly. "And you're sure that you're telling me the truth?"

"Why would I lie?"

"Well, frankly, I don't believe you. I need to know what happened that night, Carley, and from where I stand, you're the only one who can straighten things out. We can either talk this out here, or we can take a ride to the station."

I open my mouth, but no sound comes out.

He steps toward me, and I look up. "You said I wasn't in trouble."

"You won't be if you don't impede my investigation. We'll get more resolved at the station, away from distractions. Why don't you get your coat?"

I try to breathe through my nose and think of what to do. I can usually think my way out of anything, but this seems like a tall wall to climb. I know I can't turn my mother in.

"Now, Miss Connors. If you'd like to pull yourself together . . ."

I am *together*. Jerk.

". . . and answer a few questions right here, we won't have to go. But I do need answers."

I nod. Not like I have a choice.

"Good." He flips open his pad. "Okay, then. The only people in the home at the time were you, your mother, and Mr. Gray, correct?"

I nod.

"Mr. Gray was in the kitchen, and you and your mother were in the dining room."

I nod.

"You and your mother had some sort of an argument?"

"Some sort."

He glares at me. "Just *answer* the questions." He writes something in his pad. "What sort of argument did you have?"

"She tripped and blamed me."

"I see." He gives me a long, hard stare. "How did the violence begin? What was it that you did to get Mr. Gray so upset?"

I feel like I've been sucker-punched. It was me that made Dennis mad. The biggest mistake ever. I count the crisscrosses on his thin black shoelaces. One, two, three . . . I can't hear what he says exactly, but I hear something about my coat and taking a ride.

"Carley?" His tone makes me jump.

"Huh?"

"You must have said something? Or done something to get him going?"

"Well . . . I . . ."

Just then, Mrs. Murphy slides in between the cop and me. She reaches back with her right hand and takes mine. She gives it a firm squeeze.

I move closer to her.

Mrs. Murphy's tone is quiet, but boy, does she sound mad.

"How . . . *dare* you . . . come in here and insinuate that she had anything to do with what that monster did. It wouldn't matter what she did; he was the adult, and he should be held accountable for his own actions. I, for one, hope he rots in jail."

I move even closer to her.

"And you! You'd think an officer of the law would have a drop of sense . . . or compassion. What do you hope to accomplish by badgering her? She's a child and a victim, and you're treating her like a criminal. And furthermore, since she isn't a suspect, I know that you can't take her anywhere. She's staying right here . . . with *me*."

I step forward again, and the front of me almost touches her back.

His left eye squints as he stares Mrs. Murphy down. "Listen, ma'am. If you impede my investigation—"

"You listen," she interrupts. "You're not dealing with a child anymore."

He slips his notebook into his pocket but doesn't break eye contact with Mrs. Murphy. Finally he looks away first. A little thing like her stares down a guy like that.

"I'll let myself out then," he says.

"You do that," she says. We watch him open the door and leave.

She takes a deep breath and turns toward me, still holding my hand. "Are you okay, Carley?"

I try to pull my hand away, but she won't let go.

"Carley? Tell me if you're okay."

The way she stuck up for me and how she looks at me slips inside. I want to thank her. I want to ask her if my mother really held me down for that whack job. I want to ask her why she cares. I want to ask her if everything's going to be okay, because a part of me whispers that she has the answer.

"It's okay," she says, as if reading my mind. "You know he was wrong, right?" She continues. "It wasn't your fault. Not any of it."

I nod on the outside.

"Oh, that must have been so painful for you to hear, Carley."

I shrug. "Naw. It's not a big deal."

She half smiles. "Well, I guess some people would believe that line if you fed it to them."

A tiny jolt in my stomach rattles me. "I'm fine."

"Are you sure?"

"I said I'm fine." I force a smile.

"Yeah, I know." She sighs. "You're always fine."

And with that, I peel my hand away and I am gone.

I walk into the fireman room. The bed is made perfectly with little fire truck pillows. In my mind, I can see her fixing it just right. The way she lines up all the corners and makes sure the bed is straight and neat. I want to curl up on it, but it seems like a world I can never fit into.

I walk around to the other side of the bed and lie on the floor. I bring my knees to my chest and hug them. I know I will keep thinking about the horrible visit from the policeman just so I can think about how Mrs. Murphy stepped in and took my hand and wouldn't let go.

CHAPTER 14

There's No Crying in Baseball

It's been almost week since Mrs. Murphy turned that cop to dust. I have been drawn to her more, but I'm more afraid, too. Careful not to get too close.

At school I try to avoid Toni, who hates me for existing, and Rainer, who actually has a reason to wish me dead. Every time he sees me now, he calls me Oliver.

Here at the house, I pretend to do homework but really just read since I went with Mrs. Murphy and the boys to the Glastonbury library. The most amazing library ever, in a huge old white-brick house.

Mrs. Murphy has gone upstairs to tuck the smaller boys into bed, and I'm left alone with Mr. Murphy. I think he'd pack me up and mail me somewhere if he could. I watch him watch the game.

It's boring until a cute guy with dark hair and eyes comes up to bat. He looks like he plans to knock the ball into next week; I like that. He hits it by the pitcher and runs to first base. He's fast. Like me.

I'm a little startled when Mr. Murphy speaks to me. "So, you like baseball?"

"Well, I like *him*," I blurt out.

He smiles as he looks back to the screen. "Well, I like him too, but somehow I don't think in the same way you do."

I'm embarrassed.

A while later, a player from the other team hits a ball over a big green wall called "The Green Monster." I watch Mr. Murphy.

"That's just wicked great!" he says. "I knew it was time to go to the bullpen."

"Well, it makes sense to me that he hit it over that wall," I say, studying the Citgo sign that fills the sky right behind the monster.

He looks at me as if I've betrayed him.

I point at the screen. "Well, look. There's a big invitation right there. The letters in Citgo say 'See-it-go.'"

He stares at the screen for only a second before cracking up, which I like. He shakes his head. "Julie tells me that you have an interesting take on the world."

I must look worried.

"I mean it as a good thing, Carley. She says you're clever."

"She does?" I mumble.

"Yes, she does. And you know, a smart man doesn't argue with his wife!" He winks before seeming to laugh to himself.

And I decide that maybe baseball isn't so bad after all.

CHAPTER 15

Birds of a Feather

Today will be both my sixteenth day here and my birthday. I've figured that God was trying to tell me something by having me come into the world on April Fools' Day. Now, I know He was.

I was born at 9:32 a.m. Exactly at that time last year, my mother called me at school, telling the secretary it was a family emergency and that she needed to speak to me immediately.

When I got to the phone, I heard the "Happy Birthday" song sung to Carley Cakes, which was pathetic enough. But then she went into "our song," as she has called it forever.

> *We're pals together*
> *Rootin' pals, tootin' pals*
> *Birds of a feather.*

I loved it.

Today, there will be no calls. I doubt she knows where I am, but I wonder if she's awake and better and thinking of me today. She used to say it was the day she met her most favorite ever person.

I hear Mrs. Murphy scream downstairs, followed by laughing and then complaining. Mr. Murphy and the boys are laughing too, so I hurry to the kitchen. For April Fools' Day, Mr. Murphy had put an elastic band around the hand sprayer on the sink, so when Mrs. Murphy turned on the water, she got shot in the chest.

He was falling about laughing at her, but she was laughing too. She smacked him on the arm, kissed him on the cheek, and vowed revenge. A strange combination of things to do. They seemed like little kids. Something about it has stuck in my head all morning since.

I guess the Murphys don't know it's my birthday, since there were no juggling clowns in the kitchen. I'm happy and disappointed at the same time.

I'm in Ruben's class a fifth of a second when that fool Rainer asks, "Oliver? Do you want more rolls?"

I'm so sick of him that I say, "So, Rainer, what's your last name anyway? Is it Shine? 'Cause if your name is 'Rainer Shine' you could be a great mailman or maybe even a meteorologist!"

His friends laugh, but he looks mad, and I wonder if he's not going to out me when Mr. Ruben starts hitting his own desk with a pointer. "Call to order, ye peasants!"

Mr. Ruben wears a suit today. He brushes his lapel and says,

"As you can see, it's a special occasion. On this most glorious morning, I will explain the details of your term projects, which will comprise thirty percent of your final grade. I will also assign you partners."

Collective groan.

He holds up his hand. "Now, now. Hear me out." He begins to pace, rubbing his palms together. "Although everyone changes the world around them—you know, immediate family, et cetera—there are few people that have changed the world *globally.*" He spins toward us. "Now, these people have tended to be intelligent, tenacious, and good communicators, but the attribute that helped them truly succeed in their endeavors was the inclination and *ability* to kick some major backside."

There's hooting and howling.

He puts his hands up. "Yes, yes. I knew you'd like that." He points to himself. "I dressed up today in honor of these people. People like Nicolaus Copernicus, who went around spouting off silly ideas about the sun being the center of the universe—not the earth. He was criticized and thought a fool for his refusal to back off of what he believed to be fact. But now, hundreds of years later, he's known as the father of modern astronomy."

Rainer speaks up. "Does Mandy know that the sun is the center of the universe? I think she thinks it's her."

Mandy glares while the rest of the class laughs.

Mr. Ruben sobers up a bit. "Uncalled for, Mr. Tibbs."

Rainer smiles. "Hey, I'm not afraid to kick some major . . . *backside.*"

"But to what end?" Mr. Ruben laughs and holds his hands

up. "No pun intended." Then he looks at Rainer. "There's a big distinction there, now isn't there? There are different ways to change the world. I'm sure, Mr. Tibbs, that you'll change it for the better."

"By moving back to his native planet," Mandy snaps.

"Now, now, children." He leans against his desk. "We're going to focus on people that have changed the world for the good. Adolf Hitler certainly changed our world forever, but he left behind a wake of trauma and pain."

"Maybe he was mad that his parents named him Adolf," a voice adds.

Mild laughter.

Mr. Ruben continues. "But what about Anne Frank?" His body is still jumpy, but his eyes are sad. "Now, this was a girl hunted simply because she was Jewish. Hid from the Nazis for nearly two years. All the while, she keeps a diary that is published two years after the war—a war she did *not* survive. Yet she says in her diary that she still believed that man was essentially good. *That* changed the world."

A girl speaks. "I understand it was terrible and everything, but how could she change the world by just writing a diary?"

"Because she put a face to the atrocities of the Nazi death camps. She taught everyone a very poignant lesson of the dangers and horrors of war and prejudice. *And* . . . the importance of standing up for what's right and good in the world."

"Like beef jerky?" Rainer asks. No one laughs.

We stare at a picture of Anne Frank that Mr. Ruben holds up. A girl who could be in any one of our classes. She looks so happy, and I can't help but wonder if she had any idea what would happen to her. I feel embarrassed ever feeling sorry for myself when I look at her.

Mr. Ruben turns and puts the photo down on his desk. He turns back around. Slowly. "So . . . you'll choose a person that has changed the world for good. It can be from any period in history." He takes a deep breath. "Any questions so far?"

Nothing but silent, hunched-over kids.

Mr. Ruben claps loudly, and I jump. "Now for the good part." He takes a deep breath. "William Shakespeare, a man who changed the world with his quill pen, loved to write tragedy. Plays dripping with human conflict and emotion. So, in the spirit of the Bard, prepare thyselves, for I am prepared to hurl an emotional plundering."

He rubs his palms together again. "I've decided that you shall all"—he makes little quotation marks in the air—"suffer the slings and arrows of outrageous fortune." He smiles. "I've not only chosen your partners, but I've given you partners that I know you do *not* get along with or people you have little in common with."

Everyone wakes up. Including me. I can't work with Rainer. I can't.

"Oh yes! I'll do this—force you together and invite conflict—because I want you to think about what the world would be like if we all worked to understand people who are different than we are."

Rainer calls out, "I'm going to work with me, myself, and I! We don't get along, but for the good of the project . . ."

Mr. Ruben smiles. "Actually, you're going to work with Mandy Fleming."

Total relief!

Mandy slaps her desk with both hands and fumes. "That will be the day!"

"Actually, that doesn't fit your rule, Mr. Ruben," Rainer says. "There's no denying that Mandy worships me."

She whips her head around. "In your dreams."

"More like in my nightmares." He smirks.

Mr. Ruben begins. "Now, let's see. Beginning at the top of the list—Ms. Byars. You'll work with Carley Connors."

Total relief turns to panic. I am afraid to look over at her.

"It's not fair!" she says.

"Ah, yes. *It's not fair*—the mantra of teenagers everywhere." He turns to her. "That's right, my young maiden. Sometimes life isn't fair. Another lesson to be learned here."

He doles out the rest of the partnerships, and from the reactions he gets, he must really notice things about people.

CHAPTER 16

If I Throw a Stick, Will You Go Away?

The doorbell rings. I can feel my armor strengthening. This meeting with Toni over this dumb project has had my stomach in knots since it was assigned two days ago.

Toni's hair looks even blacker in the sunlight. She steps past me.

Mrs. Murphy comes into the foyer. "Well, hello. You must be Toni."

"Must be," Toni says, looking around.

Mrs. Murphy clears her throat. "Would you girls like anything to eat before you get started?"

Toni smirks. "No, thanks." She turns to me. "Let's get this over with." She heads toward the stairs and points. "Your room up there?"

"Yeah."

Toni takes three steps and turns back. "What are you waiting for? A train?"

By the time I get upstairs, I know I'm through taking garbage from Toni Byars.

I've prepared a reason for the room's decor. "I'm staying here temporarily because . . ."

"I don't care. Can we just get on with this already?" She looks upward. "God, I hate Ruben."

"We agree on that, anyway."

She sits on the bed with a bounce and opens her backpack.

"Look," I say. "Why do we have to be at each others' throats? We have to work together on this thing, and besides, I haven't even done anything to you."

"I have friends. I don't need any more."

I fold my arms. "I never said I wanted to be friends. Get over yourself."

"Can we just start this, please?" she asks.

I stare at her T-shirt. It's the one with the bright green letters that read WICKED.

"So what's with the shirt? Is this a warning to people about your personality?"

She doesn't answer.

"Are you some sort of witch or something? I'm through taking your garbage even if you do threaten to turn me into a toad."

She laughs at me and wiggles her fingers. "I'll use my special powers to turn you into a superficial bore. POOF! Hey, it worked!"

I hate her. "Look, Witchy Poo," I say. "I don't care about the grade. I'll take a zero and not blink an eye. But remember, if I take the hit—if I *refuse* to work with you—you'll take the hit too. You seem like you actually care about your grades. And I don't care what kind of freak you are." I lean toward her. "You don't scare me."

She takes a deep breath and I'm happy that she knows I have her. She looks down at a page in her notebook. "I'm not a witch, you idiot. Have you been living under a rock?"

"Yeah, basically."

She laughs in a way that makes me begin to feel foolish. "Haven't you heard of *Wicked*? It's a Broadway show. The Gershwin in New York, I might add."

"I'm sure I care."

"It's the best show on Broadway ever. My God!" She looks at me like I have a catfish coming out of my nose. "You've never heard of Elphaba?"

"What's an Elphaba?"

"Elphaba isn't an *it*. She's the Wicked Witch from *The Wizard of Oz*, and *Wicked* is the story of how she and Glinda, the Good Witch, were friends when they were younger. How they each became who they are. And Elphaba is just completely amazing."

"Figures you'd like the wicked one."

"But she's *not* wicked. She's *per*fect."

"Sounds like a rash. Like, I have a severe case of Elphaba. Oozing, pus-laden, maggot-filled . . ."

"You . . . should be struck by lightning."

"You . . . should have a flying house land on you."

"You . . . obviously don't understand."

I laugh. "I mean, call me Captain Obvious here, but do you also think Alice in Wonderland is a real person?"

"Not the same," she says, her face turning red.

"Actually, Witchy Poo, I think it is the same. Can you say *fiction*?" I lean toward her. "Say it with me, now. *Fic . . . tion.*"

We stare at each other, and she looks away first. That's one for me.

"So anyway," she begins, "who are we going to do for this wretched project? I'm thinking Stephen Sondheim or Stephen Schwartz."

"Let's make someone up that doesn't exist and convince Ruben that he does. How about . . . Jim Nasium, who brought sports to the masses . . . of Antarctica?"

I can see she wants to laugh but won't. "Stephen Sondheim and Stephen Schwartz are two Broadway musical *geniuses*. Stephen Schwartz wrote the music to *Wicked*, for God's sake. It's my dream to meet him."

"I'd like to meet Madeleine L'Engle. I guess I'm just an idiot."

"You said it, not me," she says, amused.

"Well, actually, you did say it."

She shrugs and again we stare. "Look," I say. "Some Broadway genius is no different than Rainer's pitch to do George Lucas and we all saw how thrilled Ruben was with that idea."

"He didn't say no. He just said that Rainer had to argue it well." She grunts. "Of course, Rainer couldn't argue his way into a free movie."

"Okay. That's another thing we agree on."

"Don't act like you're my friend," she says. "You have the imagination of a doorknob. Wear the right clothes, say the right things." She looks like she smells something really gross. "You're nothing. Just a little clone."

She thinks this because of the clothes Mrs. Murphy got me? I stand straight. "And you? You're obsessed with this Elephant Butt or whatever her name is!"

"Elphaba."

I'm on my guard just in case she swings. "I think I prefer Elephant Butt."

"The name Elphaba was created from the name L. Frank Baum, the—"

"Yeah, yeah. The author of *The Wizard of Oz*. You're not the only one who knows anything." I fold my arms. "Look. I couldn't care less about this. Let's just do Stephen what's-his-face. You choose. I just want to get it over with so you can take a long walk off a short roof."

"Fine," she says. "We'll do Stephen Schwartz. I already have tons of info on him."

"I'm sure you do." I laugh at her. "Elephant Butt."

We divvy up our responsibilities and agree to work separately. She leaves with the door slamming behind her, while I wonder if she is always like this. I am reminded how the flying monkeys in *The Wizard of Oz* always freaked me out no matter how many times my mother said I was being a baby.

Anyway, no monkeys. No Toni. I can finally relax.

CHAPTER 17

Bad to Worse
to Unthinkable

On Saturday morning, Daniel screams downstairs. Not a regular scream. Something that you feel in your guts when you hear it. "Mom! Come quick! There's something wrong with Michael Eric! *Mom!*"

I hear Mrs. Murphy say, "Oh my God," like someone's punched her hard in the stomach. I'm in the kitchen in a breath. Michael Eric is lying on the tile, curling his arms and arching his back. His head is pulled to the side. He shakes. Hard.

"Oh my God! Michael! Michael Eric! My honey!" Mrs. Murphy drops to her knees and holds his head. "He's having a seizure. Why is he having a seizure?"

She looks up at me, but I cannot pull my eyes from him. "Carley," she says, yanking me from my trance. "Nine-one-one *now!*"

I run to the phone and dial.

"Mommy, what's wrong with Michael Eric?" Daniel wails.

"Mom, what's wrong?" Adam sucks his thumb, which I've never seen him do.

"Nine-one-one. What's your emergency?"

I have learned to stay calm in the middle of chaos. "A little boy is having a seizure."

I answer question after question when I want to scream for them to just come.

I watch Mrs. Murphy cradling Michael Eric, rocking back and forth. Her forehead touches his. He has stopped shaking but he lies limp. Mrs. Murphy strokes his sweaty blond hair. She's pleading, "No, no, no . . ."

I tap my foot and count. Somehow I am able to count, listen, and pray all at the same time. After millions of questions, I finally hang up.

"Carley," Mrs. Murphy says through her crying. "Call Jack. Call him at the station and tell him to meet us at the hospital."

I dial the number, but another firefighter answers. "I need to speak with Jack Murphy. It's an emergency."

The man leaves the phone, and it isn't long before a panicked Mr. Murphy is on the line. "Hello?"

"Hi, Mr. Murphy. It's Carley. Michael Eric is sick. Mrs. Murphy says he's having a seizure. We called an ambulance."

"Oh my God!" His voice cuts me in half.

Mrs. Murphy's forehead touches Michael Eric's again. "Oh my God. Please . . . no." She sobs as they rock back and forth.

Daniel kneels, rubbing Michael Eric's leg. Adam stares, terrified, at his mother. Mrs. Murphy looks up at me. Her voice sounds urgent. "Tell Jack to meet us at St. Francis Hospital."

I put the phone to my ear and begin to speak. He interrupts. "I heard, Carley. I'm on my way."

When the EMTs arrive, they take Michael Eric's blood pressure, temperature, and check his eyes with a light. They listen to his heartbeat. Finally, they put him on a stretcher and wheel him out the door.

I follow the stretcher and Mrs. Murphy. A lot of the neighbors stand on their porches.

She turns around. "Carley, honey, I know you're upset. And I know you want to come, but the boys probably shouldn't be at the hospital. Would you mind staying with them? Here?"

I force myself to nod as I look past her while they load Michael Eric into the ambulance. A little bump under a white sheet on a huge stretcher.

She pats the side of my arm. "Thank you. I promise I'll call as soon as we can." She kisses each of the boys. "Don't worry. Be good. Love you." She pats the top of my arm. She turns to go.

"Wait!" I yell. "I have to get something!"

"Carley, I really have to . . ."

"Please!" I yell, already running upstairs. "Please! One second!"

I jump back down the stairs and hand Mr. Longneck to Mrs. Murphy. "Please give this to Michael Eric. He should have it."

Her smile is so sad. "I will." She gives me a quick kiss on the cheek before running to the ambulance. Her kiss has left some of her tears on my face; I reach up and touch them with my finger-tips, and I stop shaking a little.

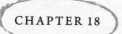

CHAPTER 18

Long Night

I watch Adam suck his thumb and wonder if he understands. I think of what Mrs. Murphy would do. I kneel. "Adam?"

He stares into my eyes but doesn't move.

"Do you know what just happened? Do you know where Michael Eric has gone?"

Without removing his thumb from his mouth, he says, "Heaven."

"No. No, Adam," I tell him. "Michael Eric has gone to the hospital, and the doctors are going to take good care of him. You'll see. He'll be home before you know it."

Daniel's voice stabs. "How do *you* know? You don't know that he'll be fine. You don't know *anything*!"

I want to smack him. Why does he always scream at me? I am ready to let him have it, but then I remember Adam. And the way he sucks his thumb. Michael Eric has to be fine. He *has* to be.

I make macaroni and cheese for dinner, but none of us eat. After a little TV, I get Adam ready for bed. I pull the covers up under his chin and ask, "Do you want me to read you a story?"

He nods, staring at Michael Eric's empty bed. I look too. "I'll be right back, okay?"

I go into the bathroom, where Daniel is brushing his teeth. Since I know he hates me, I figure I should be careful how I word this. "You know, I know that you're worried and upset, but since you're such a big guy, I am wondering if you can do something."

He talks with a mouthful of toothpaste. "Don't call me 'big guy' like I'm five. I don't need a babysitter, least of all you!"

Pegged me there. "It isn't for me. It's for Adam."

After a long pause, he looks at me through the reflection in the mirror. "What?"

"I think he'll be scared tonight. Maybe you can sleep in Michael Eric's bed so he has someone with him."

He spits into the sink. "Okay."

"Thanks, Daniel."

"I'm not doing it for you," he answers, rinsing his toothbrush.

"Yeah, I know," I mumble. Then I head back to tell Adam that his brother will sleep with him, and it's the first time that night I see him smile. We read six books, I kiss Adam on the forehead, and I say good night to Daniel.

I go down to clean the kitchen, because I know Mrs. Murphy would do that. I can't help turning around, though, to look at the phone, willing it to ring.

When I am done cleaning, I head upstairs to the fireman

room and just stand. I read the sign—the sign that greets me every time I walk in here.

BE SOMEONE'S HERO.

I walk over to the bed and I kneel down. Except for asking God to help me pass tests or keep my mother happy, I think this is the first day I've ever really prayed. "Dear God, I know that I don't pray much, and I know that sometimes you probably wonder why you made me at all, but you did your best work with Michael Eric." I look at the ceiling. "You really did. Please. Please bring him home. Amen."

I head into the room where the boys sleep and I lie on the rug next to Adam's bed. As I try to get comfortable on the floor, I realize that I've learned something I didn't know.

I love Michael Eric.

In fact, I think I love them all.

The phone rings before I'm able to fall asleep.

"Carley?" Mrs. Murphy asks.

"Yeah." I take a breath. "Michael Eric. Is he okay?"

"Yes, Carley. He's going to be fine. It was a febrile seizure caused by a fever. It has no lasting effects. Just a one-time thing. Thank God."

My muscles relax. Finally. "Oh my God. That's a relief."

She exhales. "That doesn't begin to cover it. How are the boys?"

"They're fine. They're sleeping." I turn and glance toward the boys' room. Daniel stands there, looking like he's going to lose it.

I pull the phone away from my ear. "Daniel, everything is okay. Here." I hold out the phone, and he comes quickly.

"Mom? Is Michael Eric okay?"

Silence.

"Will you tell him I say hi?"

I hear her laugh.

"When are you coming home?" He looks up at me while he listens to her. "Okay. Here she is." He hands me the phone.

"Hey, Carley! Can't talk long, but thank you so much for watching Adam. We should be out of here tomorrow about noon. Hey, can you do me a favor?"

"Sure."

"Since tomorrow is Easter, could you please put the Easter baskets out in front of the family room fireplace before the boys wake up? The stuff is on the top shelf of my closet in two shopping bags."

"No problem."

"Just do your best to figure out what is for whom. I'm sure you'll do a great job."

"Okay. Sure."

"Thanks so much, Carley."

"Okay . . ." I almost say Mom.

After Daniel goes back to bed, I find the bags. I pull out Matchboxes and figure I'll split those between Adam and Michael Eric. Next, I pull out Celtics trading cards for Daniel. I also find a Converse key chain. I'm confused by that one. Would Daniel want that? Next is a set of different flavors of lip gloss. Huh?

I lean my head into the bag. There are four baskets. Four. She has a basket for me? I can't believe that she would do that.

And it's more like Christmas than Easter as I go through the bag, finding things I know are for me. Not just random stuff either, but things I've talked about while "helping" her with dinner or things I've said I liked in stores. Mrs. Murphy really listens. But I guess I knew that.

CHAPTER 19

Paige Turner

I have dodged bullets in my life, but when Michael Eric shuffled through the front door on Easter—hugging Mr. Longneck, smiling his crooked smile—and said, "Hi, Carley," I felt like I'd dodged a meteor.

Michael Eric is supposed to lay low for the day, so we have a Sunday of movies and board games. Michael Eric and Adam have been inseparable all day; Adam has followed him everywhere. We order pizza instead of eating the roast that Mrs. Murphy had planned to make and all go to bed early—even Mrs. Murphy, who is always up late cleaning or ironing. I guess we're all still tired from thinking about what could have happened.

When I wake up for school the next day, I decide that life is too short to listen to teachers and Toni and Rainer ramble on. Besides, I'd especially like to avoid Toni since I haven't done any research on her beloved Stephen. I've had real life to worry about. She'll just have to deal.

Sometimes I wonder. On the pathetic scale, where would I land? I know other kids my age would go to the mall if they cut school, but I'm off to the library.

Problem is, I don't have a library card. But Mrs. Murphy does. I go to her purse, surprised at how loud the zipper is, and pull out her wallet. I linger on the family pictures.

I hear the squeak of the third stair down and quickly grab the library card and replace the wallet. I cough as I zip it back up. Then I take a few quick steps to the fridge. When Mrs. Murphy comes into the kitchen, I'm standing there looking for something to eat. I feel like the word *guilty* is written on my forehead.

"Big day today?" she asks me.

"Yeah, they're going to make me head cheerleader today. Because I'm so perky."

As she laughs at my joke, I feel like I should confess.

"You'd make a great cheerleader if that's what you wanted to do."

"Yeah, 'if I wanted' being the key words there." Then I start to laugh.

"What?" she asks.

"I'm thinking about a cheerleading squad yelling, 'Give me a C, give me an A . . .' and spelling my whole name . . . and then when the perkiest one yells 'What's that spell?' they'd all yell 'Outcast!'"

She laughs again; I like it that she laughs so easily. "That's right, Carley. Keep a good attitude."

I grunt and leave, forcing myself to skip the apology for deceiving the person who's been the nicest to me ever.

I arrive at the public library before it opens, so I sit with my back against the best tree in Glastonbury, happy that the leaves are starting to come back. Michael Eric and his mother love this tree. Every time we come here, he runs over to hug it. She follows, drawing her fingertips across the bark. It's like no tree I've ever seen before. Its trunk is as wide as the enormous glass doors at the library.

Once inside, I close my eyes and inhale. I love the smell of libraries, and this one is particularly nice. I look around as I walk through, wondering where I could hide if I ever needed to stay all night. I wonder how upset Mrs. Murphy would be if I disappeared. I'd probably get back to find Daniel in a party hat.

I walk up to the info desk and a librarian asks if she can help me. "Can you please tell me where the CDs are?" I ask.

She points behind herself. "Right through that doorway there."

"Thank you."

"No school today?"

She's a nosy one, but I've prepared for this question. "Oh. No, ma'am. I'm homeschooled."

She smiles. "You're a lucky girl. You must have wonderful parents."

I smile back, but I want to laugh out loud.

I run my finger along the spines of all the CDs. There it is! *The Little Mermaid*. I feel silly pulling it out, but I'm so happy. A piece

of my mother. A piece that doesn't make me sad. I turn it over and read the list of songs. There it is: "Kiss the Girl."

I spend the whole day with my nose in one book or another. I rediscover *The Cay*, a favorite book when I was young. I read right through lunch, but notice I better get moving if I'm going to be back for when the school bus would normally drop me off.

I head up to the counter with the CD and a small stack of books. She hands back the library card. "Thank you, Ms. Murphy." She smiles and looks at the screen. "Oh. You have an overdue book here. *Navigating the World of Adoption*. Shall I renew it for you?"

Talk about stunned.

"Ms. Murphy?" she asks.

"Oh, yeah. Uh, yes, please."

And although I leave with a backpack full of books, I've never felt lighter.

CHAPTER 20

Wilting Chamberlain

The fluttery feeling in my belly grows with every step. I walk back to the house in half the time it took me to get there. A Murphy? Could I really become a Murphy?

"Hey!" Mrs. Murphy says when I walk in the door. "Daniel has spring basketball tryouts. Please get ready to go."

"You know, I can stay home by myself." I realize I said *home*.

"Well, I think we need to all support each other. Big day for Daniel today."

Even though it's for the dweeb, the fluttering hasn't gone away, and I want to trap it there so it lasts and lasts. A family sticks together. I remember when she said that.

I pack enough to ensure that I don't have to watch basketball. I miss playing it, and I don't feel like cheering for *him*—probably the star athlete. Where was I when they handed out these lives?

We finally get there and sit in the bleachers. Three coaches wear warm-up suits. They hold clipboards and talk to each other like they're planning to take over the world.

Daniel looks surprisingly unhappy. Mrs. Murphy has her hands clasped underneath her chin, and her eyes are screwed into a laser look of concentration as she watches Daniel.

"Oh!" She jumps a bit and falls to a whisper. "Daniel is up."

He dribbles the ball three times, but when he looks up, the ball hits his foot and bounces off.

A kid near us says, "Looks like Murphy's been practicing," and his friend laughs.

Daniel shoots for the basket, and the ball misses the rim completely. The second one hits the rim. The third does as well. He takes ten shots and only makes one while the coaches scribble notes. How long does it take to write "Can't shoot"?

I watch Mrs. Murphy watching Daniel. She squeezes her hands together so hard that the tips of her fingers are white.

Daniel passes the ball okay, but he catches the ball like his hands are wrapped in duct tape. The kid he's with smirks every time Daniel has to run to get the ball.

Afterward, Daniel trudges over to his mother. His chin touches his chest. "I'm the absolute worst." I have to admit that I feel a little sorry for him.

"You are not! I think you did fine." She bends over to look him in the eye. "You need to lighten up on yourself, Daniel. You haven't had enough experience yet, but you'll get better."

"You're only saying that because you have to. You're my mother."

I want to tell him that being his mother doesn't mean she *has* to do anything.

CHAPTER 21

Murphy's Law

I'm sitting on the bed, staring at the cover of the *Little Mermaid* CD.

Mrs. Murphy appears in the doorway. "Mind if I come in?"

I shrug.

"What do you have there?" she asks.

Oh. "Just a CD I borrowed."

She nods, but I can tell she is thinking about something else. "You were quiet at dinner, so I wanted to check in with you. Make sure everything is okay."

I don't answer.

"Anything on your mind?"

I shrug again. Can't decide if I want to talk.

"Have you been thinking about your mom?"

I look at her quick. How did she know? I nod a little.

"Well, I'd be surprised if you weren't. That's perfectly fine, you know."

I don't think it is. I can't stop thinking about how Daniel said his mother had to say nice things because she is his mom. I keep wondering why my mother couldn't be like that. Be the "Kiss the Girl" mother all the time. How I'm so mad but I miss her, too.

"Do you want to talk?" she asks.

I shake my head. I feel like I shouldn't tell her that I miss my own mother.

"Okay, then." She stands to leave.

"You know," I blurt out, "we're only in Connecticut because my grandfather died."

"How's that?" she asks, turning back around.

"My mother inherited my grandpa's condo. She wanted to sell it off, but it was tied up in some bank thing, so we had to move in or let it go to her cousin. So we packed up everything in Vegas and drove to Connecticut."

"I see," she says slowly.

I turn to her but can't look for long. "What bothered me a lot was the funeral."

"Oh, did you really love your grandpa?"

"I didn't know him, but I heard he tried to get custody of me when I was little and that's why my mother left here in the first place."

"Oh." She purses her lips together. I know she thinks something she won't say. "So funerals are just hard, huh?"

"My mother always said he was a jerk, but he didn't look like a jerk. Of course, he *was* dead."

She half smiles.

"She said all these great things about him at the funeral."

"That must have made you feel good?"

"Naw. She looked up funeral talks on the Net. What are they called?"

"Eulogies?" she asks softly.

"Oh, yeah. She talked about a dog he didn't have and how he played tennis. He had one of those electric wheelchair things. I don't think he played tennis."

"Maybe she didn't know what to say. Eulogies are pretty rough."

God, she can find something nice to say about *anything*. "It's not right," I say. When I notice that I sound mad, I try to hide it better. "She shouldn't have done that."

She turns to me. "Why does that bother you so much, do you think?"

"Because you should never have to make up stuff about people you are supposed to love."

She talks like she's thinking out loud. "Love sure is hard to understand sometimes, Carley. But I do know that people lie for people they love all the time. A lie isn't always a bad thing. Sometimes it's a way of protecting. As long as you protect the innocent, it's okay."

I look at her.

Her voice is soft. "I would think that you would know that better than anyone else."

Mr. Murphy yells up the stairs. "Julie? Did Carley stay home from school today?"

She looks confused. "No. Why?" she answers.

Uh-oh.

Jack Murphy is angry when he comes into my room.

I stand and am on my guard, holding the CD behind my back. Proof of where I was.

"How was your day at school?" he asks.

"My day was fine."

Mr. Murphy glances at his wife and steps toward me. "I just picked up a message on the machine that says you weren't in school today."

"Well, I said I had a fine day; I didn't say it was at school."

He inhales deeply, and I can see that he's trying to calm himself down. I remind myself not to push it, but the thing is, I know he would never hurt me.

"Where were you?" he asks. Mrs. Murphy stands up, looking all disappointed. Just great.

I don't want to tell; I feel like a dork that I blew off school to go to the library. Part of me feels I ought to be more interesting. Even my mother would be disgusted.

He asks again. "Carley. Where were you today?"

"I wasn't anywhere. I didn't rob a bank. What's the big deal?"

"I can take a lot of things, but lying isn't one of them. When you went off to school without saying that you had other plans, that was a lie."

"So I should have made an announcement?"

He glares at me. Then he glances at my arm. "What are you hiding behind your back?"

"Nothing."

"Give it to me."

"No. It's mine." I don't want to have to explain why I have it.

"We don't allow drugs in this house, Carley. You put my whole family in danger."

"Drugs? Why would I have drugs?" So this is what he thinks of me? That I am a danger to his family. How can I be a Murphy if he feels this way?

Mrs. Murphy puts her hand on his shoulder. "Jack. Calm down. Carley wouldn't do that." She looks at me like she hopes she's right.

"It isn't drugs," I say, looking at Mrs. Murphy.

Mr. Murphy steps up to me. "Well, if it isn't drugs, let me have it then!" He grabs my arm. I spin and try to wrestle away but he pulls the CD out from behind my back. Then he stands, blinking.

"Pretty dangerous to the family, huh?"

"What is this?" Mr. Murphy asks.

"I was at the library."

"You skipped school to go to the library?" Mrs. Murphy asks with a slight smile.

"Yeah. Freakish, I know. Better call in the National Guard," I say, looking at him.

He looks mad but takes a step back. "I'm . . . I'm sorry. But it doesn't change the fact that you skipped school and lied about it. You're grounded for a week."

"Fine." I'm amused by this. This is the first time anyone has cared enough to ground me.

He leaves and Mrs. Murphy steps toward me. "Why did you take *this* out?" she asks.

I don't tell her it has the song that, when I close my eyes, helps me pretend that I am with my own mother. And that she loves me. A song that helps me feel the warmth on my cheek after my mother kissed me that night and how I can't remember another time like it.

But then I look at the lines on Mrs. Murphy's forehead and some of the lyrics to "Part of Your World" play in my head. I realize that the second half of that song is about the Murphys. I wonder which song I'll choose when I go to sleep tonight.

CHAPTER 22

House of Mirrors

When I step off the bus, Toni storms up to me. "You did a no-show yesterday and left me doing the work. Are you going to claim you were sick?"

I look her in the eye. "Take a breath, Witchy Poo, or you may melt."

She gets really mad and, although she makes me nervous, I hold eye contact. "Did you get in the gene pool with no lifeguard on duty?" she asks.

She has *no* idea. I turn to leave.

"You owe it to me to be here," she says.

I whip around. "I don't owe you *anything*!"

"Oh, poor Carley with her perfect little life."

"What's your *problem*? I've never done a thing to you, but you go out of your way to treat me like garbage."

"You don't have that much importance, believe me. Let's just meet at your house today and finish."

I am sick of her calling the shots. "No. Let's meet at *your* house."

She stiffens. "We can't meet at my house."

"Why not?"

She switches her backpack from one shoulder to the other. "We just can't."

I can see I have her. "We're meeting at your house or not at all."

"My mother is having a meeting there. We can't."

"What red-blooded American mother is against homework? Parents live for that stuff."

She pushes her bangs behind her ear. "Maybe yours do."

The irony makes me want to laugh, but the look on her face makes me feel sorry for her. A better person than I am would let it go, but I'm curious as to how bad it is. I wonder if Toni and I don't have some common ground after all. "I told you. Your house or nowhere."

I call Mrs. Murphy to get permission to ride on Toni's bus. I follow her off the bus as she turns up the walk of an L-shaped white house with two brick chimneys, black shutters, and a black front door. The dormers on the roof look like little separate houses. It's like a house you'd see in a movie. What was *she* so upset about?

She unlocks the front door.

"God, Toni. This house is unbelievable."

"Whatever," she mumbles.

Looking up at the high ceiling, I ask, "Do you land your plane in here?"

She doesn't answer.

"Do I need a tour guide to get from one end to the other?"

She grabs a loaf of bread.

"You hungry?" she asks. "I'm having peanut butter and fluff."

"What's that?"

"Wow, Connors. You really have been living under a rock, haven't you?"

Duh.

She slaps something together and hands me a sandwich with white stuff oozing out of the sides. Reminds me of the caulk that Mr. Murphy redid the tub with. "Looks yummy."

"Just try it."

"Are you sure you're not poisoning me?"

She leans against the counter as if she really considers it. "You won't know until you eat it, now will you?"

I'm surprised at how good it is. Sweet and creamy. "So this is how rich people eat, huh?" I ask, licking my sticky fingers.

"C'mon. Let's go upstairs," she says with her mouth full.

"Can I have some milk?" I ask.

"Geez, Connors. Anyone ever tell you you're high maintenance?"

"Yeah, actually," I say, remembering that my mother had a much worse way of putting it.

Toni is putting the milk back when a door closes off to the side of the kitchen. "Oh, great," she mumbles.

A woman comes into the kitchen carrying four shopping

bags. She is tall and pencil shaped. Her hair is wavy and dark and she wears a blue suit. Her teeth are freakishly white.

"Oh, you have a little friend over?"

Toni grunts. "Yeah, we were just about to play ring-around-the-rosy."

The woman's face turns to stone. Then she turns to me, scans me, holds out her hand, and says, "Sarah Byars. So very nice to meet you."

I take her hand, which gives me the creeps. "Nice to meet you too," I lie.

"Toni," she says. "Don't you like the vibrant color of her shirt?" Her voice is sweet, but I get the feeling she could spit icicles. "Nothing wrong with a little color."

"C'mon," Toni says, picking up her backpack and heading for the stairs. "We have work to do."

Toni leads me up to her room. Her carpet is bright green, and the walls are sponge-painted in a similar shade.

"Did Oscar the Grouch explode in here or what?"

She laughs. "It's green in honor of Elphaba." She points at me. "And don't start or I'll seriously . . . seriously hurt you."

I believe her.

Posters of Broadway shows plaster the walls. There's a pointed witch's hat on the post of her bed. Her comforter is green and shiny. Okay. She really is obsessed.

She unzips her backpack. She is so much quieter—sadder. She looks upward. "I wanted to do the ceiling green, but my dad said no."

"You have a dad?" I blurt out.

"Yeah, Connors. I have a dad. Ever take biology?"

"Yeah. I mean, I know that but . . . I mean . . ."

Toni piles books on her desk. "What's *wrong* with you, Connors?"

I shrug, afraid to say anything out loud.

"My dad is awesome," Toni says, "but he works in Japan mostly, so I hardly ever see him. It's been thirty-two days now."

So she counts the days away from her father while I count the days away from my mother.

She looks up at the wall. "He helped me do these walls, even though my mother complained that it didn't fit the flow of the house."

"Houses flow?"

"Precisely," she says, rolling her eyes.

"I'm sorry I forced you to come to your house today."

She doesn't say anything, but I catch her glancing at me.

I think she must feel like she's given something away, bringing me here and telling me about her father. I say, "I promise that we'll ace this project, okay?"

She half smiles. "Whatever you say, Connors."

"Whatever I say?"

"Forget it."

After an awkward silence, I ask, "So, are you in the drama club at school?"

"Oh, you mean the *trauma* club? No way. I go to acting camp in the city, though. Every summer since forever. My dad promises to sign me up with a voice coach, too."

"Cool." I sit on her bed and bounce, studying the Broadway posters. "So how many of these shows have you seen?"

"Actually," she says, looking around, "I've seen them all. Fortunately, my mother is all about culture too, so she takes me to all the New York shows. I especially love musicals. They're all different—like people."

"I've never seen a musical. I mean on stage."

"You're kidding!" She clasps her hands and her eyes spark. "Broadway is amazing! There isn't any other place like it. One of the shows we saw, *The Drowsy Chaperone*, talked about how everything works out in musicals. And it's the only place a person can burst into song without being labeled a weirdo."

I want to tell her that anyone bursting into song *would* be a weirdo, but instead I say, "I guess it might be cool to see one sometime."

"Ask your mom. She'd go."

I burst out laughing. "Are you kidding me? No way."

She looks puzzled, so I change the subject. "So, *Wicked* is your favorite?"

"Totally. It's the best, and Elphaba is my favorite character."

"You said it's about *The Wizard of Oz*? I mean, don't throw a chair or anything, but it sounds dumb."

"You'd have to see it to understand."

"Try me."

She takes a deep breath. "Do you . . . ?" Her mouth kind of twitches like she can't decide whether to say it or not.

"Yeah?" I ask.

"You wouldn't understand. Look at you, for God's sake!"

"What?" I ask.

"You're like Glinda."

I crack up. "The good witch? Uh, I don't think so."

She looks sad. "Do you ever feel like you . . . don't fit in? Like everyone else gets something you don't?"

"God, yeah." She has *no* idea.

"But do you ever think that maybe . . . it's not you who is off base but other people? That people label you as something you aren't?"

"Yeah." My own voice sounds far away. I think back to all the times people assumed I was dumb because I had mismatched or dirty clothes. My science teacher accused me of plagiarism because my paper was "too good."

"Well, it's like that with Elphaba," Toni says. "She's ostracized because she's green. And she's labeled wicked when she isn't."

"I know what it's like to be labeled like that," I say slowly. "I met someone once who drew all these conclusions about me based on the clothes I wear. A clone, I think she said."

Toni lets out a little laugh as if to say, well, what do you know? She folds her arms and leans back against her pillow.

"What?" I say. "Speechless? We should throw a parade."

"Okay, Connors. I get it." She sits up fast. "But look at you! I mean, why do you want to look like everyone else?"

"Because I never have before."

Toni looks puzzled again but says, "Well I, for one, would rather fail miserably at being unique than just be another clone. Like my mother."

"She didn't seem *that* bad."

"She's like cardboard. Superficial," Toni says. "Deeply shallow, as they say in *Wicked*."

"Fully empty," I add.

She laughs. "Yeah. It wouldn't matter to her if you were a serial killer as long as you wore the right clothes."

"So . . . you think she doesn't like you?"

She looks shocked but talks fast. "I think I'm the only thing in her life that doesn't fit the perfect picture, and she wishes that she'd had a different daughter." Her eyes are wide at first; then she closes them like it hurts to look at anything.

I kind of want to tell her about my mother, but I don't want her labeling me as the pathetic foster kid. A throwaway; who'd want to be friends with someone like that?

"Hey," I say to Toni, who now stares at her green carpet. "Is your mom going to be downstairs when I leave?"

"I guess."

I laugh. "Turn around."

"Why?"

"Just trust me," I say. "Turn around and don't look until I tell you."

She does. I take off my shirt really fast and put it back on inside out and backward. The tag of the shirt is on the front now. "Okay. Turn around."

She does.

"Am I ready for one of your mother's fancy lunches, or what?"

Toni Byars finally smiles.

CHAPTER 23

Truth Hurts, Huh?

Back at the Murphys', Daniel is tormenting himself with that basketball again. I'm feeling brave, so I go out.

"Hey, Daniel. How's it going? How about a little one-on-one?" I ask.

"I'm practicing."

"No better practice than getting your butt kicked by me, right?"

He glares.

"C'mon. I'll take it easy on ya."

"I don't want to. I'm practicing. Besides, the teams aren't fair."

"So what?"

"Go play in the road."

"Harsh." I laugh at him. "I'm just trying to help you."

He grits his teeth. "Leave me alone. No one asked you."

"Look. You're a wussy mama's boy, I know. The truth hurts."

He stops and turns. "Well, at least I have a mother." He glares. "Truth hurts, huh?"

He won't get me with that again. I remind myself not to get mad.

He dribbles but the ball hits his foot and rolls into the grass. He glares at me like it's my fault.

"Look, Daniel." I fold my arms. "It just so happens that I was the high scorer on my basketball team back home." Okay, this is a stretch. But I was pretty good. "I want to help you."

"Why?" he asks, picking up the basketball.

"I really don't know. But I am willing to help you if you want. I'd kind of . . . like a truce, I guess."

He turns the ball over in his hands. Probably thinking about how he may be making a deal with the devil.

He begins to dribble. I go over, steal it easily, and go in for a layup.

He folds his arms. "Give me my ball back."

I stand, smiling. "Come get it."

He can't get it from me. I dribble and talk to him at the same time. "Look. See how I dribble really close to the ground? You dribble as high as your neck, which screams, 'Come steal the ball from me.' Also, it's harder to control that way. The closer to the ground, the better."

I hand him the ball. "I'll try to take it from you now." I go for the ball but never actually take it. Whenever I move in to get it, he finally learns to shorten his dribble.

When he stops to take a squirt from his water bottle, I ask him, "Doesn't your dad practice with you? He's obsessed with sports. He must love this stuff!"

His face darkens. "Not really."

"Why?"

"My dad loves baseball and wants me to play that, but I just don't want to." He looks into my face without hatred for the first time ever. "It's just that I *love* basketball. I love to watch it and play it. Baseball is boring to me. You stand in the outfield and do nothing for most of the time." He bounces the ball once. Hard. "Do you know what my middle name is?"

I shake my head.

"Dale. As in Dale Murphy, this amazing baseball player from before I was even born. My name is Daniel Dale Murphy because my father planned, from the time I was born, that I would play baseball. He's so mad that I don't. I hate it."

"He probably doesn't mind that much. He seems like the kind of guy that would like all kinds of sports—a real jock type. Have you even asked him?"

"My father says that baseball is the thinking man's game and basketball is for morons. He's such a jerk about it that even if I liked baseball—which I don't—I could never play it."

I am shocked he told me this. I'm even more shocked that the Murphys aren't perfect after all.

CHAPTER 24

Bagged

Today, we have a social studies field trip to Mystic Seaport. Whatever it is, it sounds better than being in school. I get on a bus, wondering which would be worse, sitting with a jerk or sitting alone.

"Hey, Connors," Toni calls.

Relieved, I fall into the seat next to her, holding my bagged lunch. I try to hide Mrs. Murphy's handwriting on the bag. "Carley Connors, Period 1." I love sitting here, feeling just like everyone else. Normal.

Mr. Ruben steps onto the bus with what looks like a band uniform and a tricornered hat and most of us laugh. "Good morning, ye lads and lasses! As you can see, I am your captain!" he says in a bold voice.

"Aye-aye, Captain!" Rainer says to Mr. Ruben. Always the suck-up.

The bus driver pulls out of the driveway. Mr. Ruben is holding sheet music, thinking that we'll all sing sea shanties. He has a better chance of getting this bus to land on Mars.

Once on the road, Toni asks, "So, that's some lunch you've got there. You carrying a full Thanksgiving meal or what?"

I think about how nice Thanksgiving would be at the Murphy house. I shrug.

"How can you not know what's in your own lunch?" she asks.

"I didn't pack it."

"Seriously, Connors? Your mother still makes your lunch?"

Change the subject. "Where is your lunch?"

She pats her pocket. "Right here. Two Andrew Jacksons will take me through lunch and to the gift shop."

My mother used to quiz me on which presidents are on money. "You've got forty bucks for lunch?"

"Sure, Connors," she says. She leans over and looks at the writing on my bag. Here comes the teasing. "So open the bag. Let's see what you've got."

I guess she must be hungry. I open the bag and pull out a turkey sandwich, red grapes, banana bread, Fruit Roll-Up, and two juice boxes at the bottom. There is a note too. "Have fun. Be safe. Love, Mrs. M."

"Mrs. M?" she asks.

"That stands for Mrs. Mom. A joke we have." I pause. "I know. It's dumb."

"Does she write notes like that a lot?" Toni asks.

"Yeah. She likes notes. She leaves sticky notes over the sink and stuff. Kind of sappy stuff."

Toni is quiet, turning to stare out the window.

"So, have you been to Mystic before?" I ask.

"Yeah. Lots of boats. Thrill a minute. Lunch counter isn't bad, though. Burgers and fries."

"Really?"

She turns toward me. "Soda too. Listen, Connors. I'll do you a favor. How about I buy your lunch off of you for twenty bucks? Then you'll have money for the lunch counter and gift shop."

"Are you kidding me? Sure!" I take the note out and hand her the bag.

"No. You have to leave the note."

"But why would you want that?"

"It's part of the lunch, Connors. That's why."

I stare at it. I really want it. But twenty bucks is so much money. "Okay, deal!"

She starts digging through the bag. Eating grapes. Reading the note. "You're all right, Connors," she says.

CHAPTER 25

Mrs. Murphy's Big Idea

So," Mrs. Murphy asks, "do you have any plans for the weekend?"

"Yeah. Running with the bulls in Spain, maybe . . . photographing polar bears. Same old boring stuff."

She chuckles. "I've been thinking."

"Sounds dangerous," I say.

She points at me with a spatula and a slight smile. "Watch it there, kid."

"Why? You going to flip me?" I say, pointing at her weapon.

She shakes her head. "What a clip."

There's another one.

"So, do you like that Toni girl? Would you say . . . that you're yourself around her? I always think that's the true measure of how good a friend is."

I think that I am comfortable around her now—except that

she doesn't know who I really am. I've been thinking I should tell her. But I'm afraid she'll change her mind about me. I'm not sure how to answer Mrs. Murphy.

"She's . . . not into stuff you shouldn't be into, right?"

"Actually, she is."

Mrs. Murphy looks concerned.

"Broadway musicals. A sickness."

Mrs. Murphy laughs and turns back toward the sink. "Why don't you invite her over for dinner tomorrow. Would you want to do that?"

"Uh, I can ask her, I guess."

"You sound nervous."

Funny how she does that. Knowing what I'm thinking. "Maybe a little." I shrug.

"Can't hurt to ask!" she says.

I'm not so sure . . .

Toni steps into the kitchen with a plate of brownies. "Here you go," she says to Mrs. Murphy. "My mom sent these."

"Brownies!" Michael Eric and Adam yell.

"After dinner. Not before," Mrs. Murphy says, holding the plate out of their reach.

Michael Eric looks at me but points at Toni. "Which super-hero is she?"

Toni laughs. "You guys have high expectations here."

I bend over and look Michael Eric in the eye. "No superheroes now. Maybe later, though. Okay?" He goes back to a pile of blocks with Adam.

"So," Mrs. Murphy begins. "You two can hang out upstairs or watch TV since Jack is at the station tonight. Whatever you'd like!"

I know we'll get no peace down here. "You want to hang out in my room?"

"Sure," she says, and we head upstairs. "I'd forgotten this nice room, Connors!" Toni says when we walk into the fireman room.

I guess this would be a good time to tell her the truth, but I'm not in the mood to answer questions. The questions about why I'm here. What harm can it do to just pretend a little longer? "Well, my mom said I could have a bigger room, so I'm staying in Michael Eric's while it's being painted." I feel bad about the lie.

"I say you fight to keep this one, Connors." She laughs as she falls back on my bed.

"So what's Rainer's story, anyway?" I ask.

She bolts up. "Rainer? Oh my God! We've known each other forever. I mean forever. Our mothers are both totally caught up in the Junior Women's League. Total do-gooders . . . on the outside, anyway."

"What's a junior woman?" I ask.

She cracks up. "Very funny, Connors."

Except I was serious.

"So, what's the deal? Why is he always giving you a hard time? Like calling you Oliver? And what's a roll stuffer?"

"Who knows," I lie.

"Maybe he stands too close to the ovens at his parents' restaurant. They have him working there all the time. I mean, all. The. Time." She laughs, retying her shoe. "He's such an idiot! And he talks tough but you can put him in his place pretty easily. I even beat him up in the third grade."

"You did?"

"And the fifth."

"Really?" I crack up.

"Yeah, and he's still nervous I'm going to hit him. I can tell." Toni bounces on my bed. "So, enough about that twit, Connors! Ask me anything!"

"Uh . . . why do you always call me Connors?" I ask.

"I said you can ask me anything. I mean anything on the planet. And that's the best you can come up with?"

"I'll try to do better."

She seems amused. "Well, speaking of names, here's something interesting, Connors. Actually . . . I gotta tell you. My name isn't Toni. Not really, anyway."

"Huh? What is it then?"

"If I tell you, you swear on a thousand souls you won't tell anyone?"

"It depends on the souls."

"I'm not telling you then."

"Okay, fine. A thousand souls."

She looks toward the ceiling and attempts an angelic face. "Charity."

"*Charity*? That's your name? Charity Byars? Oh my God. No wonder you changed it!"

She sits up straight and her whole face lights up. "I've gotta tell you, Connors, when Idina Menzel won the Tony Award for Elphaba, I swore that someday I'd have a Tony Award with my name etched on the front. But I can't have 'Charity Byars' etched on anything!"

"Charity? Really?" I ask.

"At least your last name isn't *Case*."

"Yeah, you're right." She laughs. "Anyway, my mother, the perfect one, had this idea that I would grow up to be her Mini-Me. She just about keeled over when I told her she could keep the name Charity. That I was going to be called Toni in honor of my future award. Not only that, I'm going to make millions on Broadway and keep every penny."

"Somehow, I have a feeling you *will* make millions on Broadway."

"Then split it with my best friend? Is that the next thing out of your mouth, Connors? Because you can forget it. I'm not giving you a dime!"

I guess she'll think that I'm upset about not getting a cut of the millions when I'm really trying to believe that she called me her best friend.

CHAPTER 26

Walk Off Loss

I plop down on the couch. "So," I say to Mr. Murphy. "The Sox are down by two points?"

"Yeah, but you say *runs*, not *points*." He frowns at the TV.

"Oh." I am nervous now. He sounds angry.

I've been wondering about him and the adoption book. I figure that if Mrs. Murphy took out the book, she must be okay with the idea, but I wonder if he will go for it. If he likes me at all.

He is sitting on the edge of the couch, resting his elbows on his knees. The Yankees have the bases loaded with no outs. The guy at bat has a "2" on his jersey; how intimidating can he be with a number like that?

Number two hits the ball and ends up with a double. Mr. Murphy slaps his leg. "You're kidding me!" he yells. I'd like to ask what the attraction is of watching it if it makes him miserable.

The doorbell rings. Mrs. Murphy answers it, and Toni comes around the corner. I meet her in the kitchen.

"Hey, Connors! What's up?" Toni asks, smiling.

"Ceiling," I say.

Mrs. Murphy laughs.

"You think you're pretty funny, don't ya, Connors? Don't get a swelled head 'cause your mother laughs. She probably thought what you left in your diapers was a masterpiece."

With the word *mother*, Mr. and Mrs. Murphy look questioningly at me. It's bothering me that I haven't told Toni the truth. The more I like her, the more my silence feels like a lie.

Toni's attention turns toward the TV. She walks in that direction, stepping just inside the family room. "Yup," Toni says. "There is nothing better than baseball on a Sunday afternoon. My dad and I watch it whenever he's home."

Mr. Murphy looks like he's ready to adopt her. Maybe she'll win me some brownie points if she's sitting around talking about the wonders of the blessed Red Sox.

"And there's nothing better," she continues, "than watching the Red Sox get pummeled into dust by the Yanks. Don't you love a team that goes eighty-six years without winning a Series and, when they finally do, they act like they own baseball?"

Okay. In my mind, I see this whole thing as a car teetering on a cliff. Rocking back and forth.

"Losers," she says. "Sox fans are nothing but losers."

And the car goes over. Falling and falling.

Mr. Murphy's head turns . . . slowly . . . and he glares up at her as if she has just pulled out a gun. She finally gets around to looking at him. Noticing his Red Sox hat and the Dropkick Murphys shirt. "Oh," she says. "Sorry."

I have never imagined Toni retreating from anyone, but she is out of there in a shot. Back in the kitchen with me and Mrs. Murphy.

"I have a few things to say about Yankees fans," he yells at us.

"Now, Jack." Mrs. Murphy is amused. "Remember you're the adult here."

"You really have a way with people," I say to Toni.

"Well, I won you over, didn't I, Connors? And you were pretty rough stuff that first day we met. Downright terrifying, I'd say." She laughs. "Actually, you looked more like you were going to pee your pants."

She's right, and I hate thinking of myself as a coward. It bothers me how even though I act brave, things still scare me on the inside. "Listen, Byars," I say. "I could take you any day of the week. And if I think back to the way things really happened, I did. Terrifying is right. You better believe it."

"God, Connors. You're beginning to sound like me."

"I hear there are psychiatrists for that kind of thing."

"Nice, Connors. Real nice." Toni smirks.

Mrs. Murphy is at the sink now; sometimes I think she's chained to it. Daniel comes in, dribbling his basketball, and his mother asks him to stop.

While Daniel goes to the fridge for a Gatorade, Michael Eric and Adam drag a bag of cars into the kitchen.

"Boys, can't you find another place? I'm working here," Mrs. Murphy says, cutting up green peppers.

"But Mom," Michael Eric says, "you're always working, and we need the lines for roads."

At first I don't know what he means and then I see Adam setting up Matchbox cars on the grout lines of the tile.

She sighs but lets it go.

"So, Connors," Toni says. "Will your mom let you go for a walk or something before dinner?"

Mom? I panic. I have to cut this off before . . .

Michael Eric looks up. "Is Carley's mommy here?"

Toni looks like she feels sorry for Michael Eric. Like he has oatmeal for brains.

"C'mon," I say. "Let's shoot hoops." I turn to go, praying that she will follow.

"Well? Is she?" Michael Eric stands. "Is she here to take Carley away?"

Hearing him say that and looking at his big, blinking eyes gets to me, but I shake it off. "Michael Eric, you're such a joker." I look toward Mrs. Murphy. "So is it okay if I go?" I ask her.

She turns toward me and looks sad, and I want to be able to freeze everyone else in time and ask her why. Because I'm a liar? Or because she'd like me to be her daughter? Or because the thought is so terrible that it makes her cry?

"Don't go far," she says. And for her, that's a perfect answer. It says *yes, but I'm worried about you.*

I turn to go and Toni does, too. I can tell she thinks something is weird, but what really shocks me is that Daniel hasn't outed me.

I hear Michael Eric running, coming up behind me. Before I can say anything, he's wrapped his arms around my leg and is laughing. "Carley! Carley! Your mom is my mom? And your dad is my dad, too? And you're gonna stay here with us for always?"

Daniel finally lets out a small burst of laughter. "I can't believe you didn't tell her."

"Daniel. Not your business," Mrs. Murphy says. She is already coming toward us.

"Wait," Toni says, with one eye practically closed. "She's not your mother? Is she an aunt or something?"

Daniel folds his arms and laughs again, and his mother shoots him a glare that shuts him off.

"No!" Michael Eric says. "Carley is from the Fosters!"

"No, Michael Eric," a red-faced Mrs. Murphy says. "Not from the Fosters." She puts her hand on the side of his face and bends over to look him in the eye. "Go back to your cars now. Okay, pal?"

Toni's face is red now, too, as if she's been the victim of a practical joke.

I search my head for something. *Anything.* To explain. Because I wasn't just silent. When I called the Murphys "Mom" or "Dad" I was lying; I just really liked the sound of it.

"End the agony already," Daniel says. "Tell her you're a foster kid."

She turns to me. "You're a foster kid? This isn't your family?"

That hurts. "Toni, I . . ."

Her eyes narrow. "You lied to me? About who you are? Is your name even Carley Connors, or is that a big fat lie too?"

"I'm sorry, Toni. I never meant to lie. But being a foster kid . . ." I swallow hard and try to count as I speak. "Being a foster kid is just so . . . you can't believe how . . . humiliating it is . . . and I . . ."

Daniel doesn't look amused anymore, and his mother looks like she's going to cry. And I want to run. But I know I can't. I have to stand and take it this time.

"I didn't know what you'd think of it," I plead. "I'm still *me* . . . Please, Toni. You're my best friend."

"I'm so *dumb*!" She makes two fists. "I told you everything about me and you just . . ." She steps away from me. "See ya, Jane Doe, or whoever you are."

As I'm trying to get my head around the Jane Doe comment, she spins and bolts out the door.

The Murphys all look at me. But I can't look at them, so I study the white threads on my high tops. The last three letters in "friend" are "end." If you take out the "n" you get "fried."

Mrs. Murphy moves toward me, and I back quickly into the wall, hitting my head on the door frame.

I was right about being a foster kid. It is humiliating.

"Oh, Carley," she says in that voice that I just can't hear now. "It's . . ."

"Yeah, whatever," I say, cutting her off. And I run upstairs to the fireman room, close the door, crawl under the bed, say a prayer that she won't come looking for me, and hope that Toni will forgive me.

For a few seconds, I even try to cry. But I can't.

CHAPTER 27

Irish Abyss

Mrs. Murphy pops her head in to ask, "Hey, Carley. Got a minute?"

I've been lying in bed for two hours, listening to Ariel sing about how she doesn't belong anywhere.

"Sure," I answer, sitting up.

I can tell by her face that something serious is on her mind. I scroll through all the things it could be. Is she going to tell me I'm going to be adopted as a Murphy? Is my mother here? Is Toni dressed as Elphaba at the front door, waiting to turn me into a gnat?

"Carley?" Mrs. Murphy asks, pulling me out of my zone. She laughs a little.

I am on guard. "What's so funny?"

"Jack goes off into those little dazes too. I call it the Irish abyss. Always deep in thought about something, you Irish."

I like being labeled with something that has to do with the Murphys.

"Well, Carley, I'm wondering how you're doing. That whole thing with Toni must be very upsetting for you."

I nod.

"She obviously cares for you. I think she'll come around. Perhaps you can talk to her?"

"I don't think she'll talk to me."

"Well, you don't know that until you try."

"I don't need to jump out of an airplane to find out what would happen."

"You're pretty funny, Carley. But I know this is serious to you. She's a good friend and those are hard to come by. Perhaps it's worth taking the risk. Talk to her when you can. I bet she'll listen to reason."

I hope she's right.

I eat more chicken casserole than usual. Every time I get the feeling that I want to say something, I stuff my mouth with food.

Michael Eric has fallen out of his chair for the third time and I can tell Mrs. Murphy has had it. "Michael Eric, if you can't sit at the table like a big boy, then you'll have to leave it."

"Okay," he says, jumping out of his chair. "That cancer-role is yucky anyway."

"*Casserole*," Adam corrects him. "You're so dumb."

"Am not! You're dumb!" Michael Eric screeches.

"Well, you smell like a butt!"

"That's enough out of the two of you!" Mr. Murphy says with

his mouth full. "I think Mom's dinner is delicious and if any of you fellas don't want to eat it, well, that means there's more for me!" He smiles and winks at his wife across the table, but his forehead is covered with lines.

"Michael Eric, sit down," Mrs. Murphy says.

"But Mommy, you said I could leave," he whines.

"That's not exactly what I said. Sit."

"You did!" he yells. "I don't wanna eat yucky dinner! I wanna play!"

Mrs. Murphy gets up and grabs Michael Eric by the arm and sits him back in the chair. He's crying and his face is blotchy and red.

Mr. Murphy's tone is even lower than usual. "Julie, calm down."

She gets up and storms out. The downstairs bathroom door slams. Adam starts sobbing. Mr. Murphy stands up, wipes his mouth, and musses Adam's red hair. "It's okay, pal." Then he drops his napkin on the table and heads for his wife.

Daniel says, "This is your fault, Michael Eric."

Michael Eric screams, "Is not! It's yours, dumb face!" I feel like I'd better get things calmed down somehow.

I look at Michael Eric and Adam with their blotchy, wet faces. "I tell you what. I'll play superheroes with you guys if you can be quiet. And I'll give my dessert to the one who's the quietest."

Michael Eric and Adam are happy about this, but Daniel says, "I don't want your dumb dessert."

Michael Eric's face scrunches up and he sticks out his tongue at Daniel. I can't ignore the hushed words between Mr. and Mrs. Murphy in the bathroom.

"You know, guys, I'm gonna go see if everything is okay." After all, they don't know that I'm in their category and should stay put. "Remember. Quietest gets dessert."

"Big whoop," Daniel mumbles. He gets up, walks into the family room, and turns on the TV.

I tiptoe into the hallway and stand beside the bathroom door.

"I'm worried about you, Julie. You're spread way too thin with this girl. Our boys need you to be their mother."

I hear her crying.

"Look, Julie. I like Carley; you know I do. And I know how much you love her, but she isn't ours . . ."

I lean against the wall. She *loves* me?

"She'll be going back to her own mother. You have to accept that."

"We don't know that for sure."

"Oh no, Julie. We *do* know she's going back . . ." He moves toward the door, so I move away. Then, I can't hear what else he is saying.

Then I hear her yelling. "*Jack . . . Murphy*! I'm so sick of the world revolving around you and what you need!"

I get away just before she barrels out and heads into the kitchen. She goes to the sink, leans her hands against the counter, picks up a mug, then throws it into the sink. Pieces fly everywhere.

The boys freeze, only moving when they look at each other. Michael Eric cries and holds Mr. Longneck to his chest. Then Adam. Things are going to go bad, I can feel it.

She turns to the boys. "Hey, guys. Everything is okay. Mommy is just upset, but everything is okay. I'm not upset because of you."

It's *me*.

Mr. Murphy comes back into the kitchen. He doesn't say anything, but he stands kind of like one of the boys when they're in trouble. A side of him I didn't know about. "Julie?"

"Not now, Jack. Just leave me be."

The boys freeze up again. So do I, but I can see she's calming herself down. My mother couldn't do that to save the world.

"I'm going to take a shower," she says, and leaves. Soon, Mr. Murphy heads upstairs.

I sit with the boys for a few minutes before they go play with Legos. I clear the table and have everything just about cleaned up when Mrs. Murphy appears.

She has a soggy ponytail. She looks younger somehow.

"Carley?" she asks, looking around the kitchen. "Did you do all of this by yourself?"

"Yeah," I say, worried.

"You didn't have to do that," she says, looking like she's really glad I did.

"I don't mind. It's the least I can do."

And I think about Mr. Murphy and how he doesn't want to keep me here anymore. Although he never acts that way; he is always nice to me. I like him, and wish that he liked me more. I can't take the thought of being sent away again, but I don't think Mrs. Murphy would fight her husband to keep me here.

CHAPTER 28

Must . . . Get . . . Out . . . Now

I can't take it anymore. The Murphys. *Julie* Murphy, to be precise. I've hung a question mark on her, and I don't know what to do. Seems like I'm afraid to trust her anymore. Or maybe I want to leave before I'm told I have to go. All I know is . . .

I have to get out.

I pick up the phone and dial the number on the card. Mrs. MacAvoy's number.

The phone rings one, two, three, four times. She must know it's me.

I get her voice mail, and I hang up.

I redial. This time I'll leave a message.

The phone rings again, and I get a real voice. Oh no.

"Hello?" she asks. "Hello?"

"Uh, hi?" I say.

"Yes? Who is this?"

"Carley. Carley Connors. I'm sorry. I must have the wrong number." I slap my forehead. That was *so* dumb.

"Oh, Carley Connors. Of course. Is there anything wrong?"

"I need to get out," I say. I want to reach out and grab the words back, wondering if this is one of those times when I shoot myself in the foot and can't explain why, or if I really want to leave the fireman room, chicken casseroles, playing superheroes with Michael Eric and Adam, or sitting on the kitchen counter, talking to Mrs. Murphy. I decide that I am an empty-headed twit.

"What's happening, Carley? Are you in danger?"

"Uh, no. I just called to say hello."

"You did, did you?"

"Yeah. So how are you?" I try to sound happy.

"You just said that you had to get out. What did that mean?"

"Oh. I . . . uh . . . meant that I need to get out more. You know. Fresh air. And stuff." I shake my head. I sound like a moron. "Mrs. MacAvoy, everything is fine. Really. So, how are you anyway?"

She takes a sip of something. "Assuming that everything is fine, I could be happier. Because with all the things that I have to do already, now I have to fit visiting *you* into my schedule."

"No, you really don't have to do that."

"Our policy is that if a client calls, we need to make a home visit."

"Even if I just called to say hello?"

"Yes, Carley. A child can call in crisis but not be able to tell the truth on the phone. Is that what's happening? Are you in crisis, but someone is there watching you? I can send the authorities immediately."

Now I worry that I'll get the Murphys in trouble.

"Carley? Are you there?"

"Uh, yeah. Sorry."

"So is everything okay? Are you in any danger?" She actually sounds nice.

I'm in all kinds of danger, but it's my own doing. "No, everything is fine. Really."

"Okay, then." She sighs. "I understand it isn't an emergency, but I'll have to see you soon nevertheless."

"Please don't do that."

"Hey, Carley. You called me, remember?"

"Yeah."

"Okay, then. I'll see you soon."

Soon? What's soon? Just when I thought I couldn't mess things up any more, I do.

CHAPTER 29

Friend or Fiend?

At school Toni acts as if she's never spoken to me ever. She sits in Ruben's class in another seat, and when I call her name at the end of the period, she bolts.

I'm surprised how much I miss hanging out with her. Even on the days she never shut up.

I follow her out of Ruben's room. I must be desperate because I know how this will end. But I have to try anyway.

"Toni! Please wait!"

She doesn't turn around but does speed up. I jog past her and turn to stand in front of her. She stops, spins, and walks the other way. I drop my backpack and move in front of her again. "Just let me explain," I plead.

This time when she turns away, I reach out without thinking and grab her arm. She whips around. "Touch me again, and I'll remove your fingers for you." She sounds angry but looks like she could cry. I'm really shocked. And feel terrible.

"Leave me alone, Connors." She storms off, but I follow.

She pushes open the door to the faculty bathroom. I hesitate and then follow. No one is in there, thank God.

"You owe it to me to listen."

She whips around. "Oh, that's ironic coming from you. Talking about what I *owe* you. What do I owe you, Carley? The truth? How about the truth?"

"You're right. I should have told you. But I was afraid."

"Afraid of what? I told you everything. *Everything*. I told you about my dumb name and my lousy mother and my father who doesn't care enough to answer my e-mails half the time. I never kept anything from you."

I never knew her dad didn't answer her e-mails.

Her voice gets louder as the hallways empty outside. The bell has rung and everything is quiet. Toni stares at the floor, and the only thing I can hear is her trying to catch her breath. "Carley, I trusted you. Every day you talked about your mom and dad and brothers. Every day was a lie."

"I'm sorry."

"I'm so sick . . ." She holds in her crying; I know that look. "I'm so *sick* . . . of people telling me one thing and being another. When will someone just tell me the *truth*? I thought you were different." She motions toward my clothes. "Even with this hopeless wardrobe of yours, I thought you were the real deal. I thought you were my friend."

"You're right. I'm a jerk. A liar. I don't deserve another chance, but please give me one. Please. I'll never, ever lie to you ever again."

"Yes, you're all those things. At least you're being honest for once."

I yell. I'm surprised, but I do. "Fine, then. Great. Listen. You go on endlessly about Elphaba and how great she is and how everyone judges her on how she looks and it isn't fair. You do the same thing, Toni! The same thing."

"What are you talking about?"

"You talk about my hopeless wardrobe as if I'm wrong because it's different than yours. I haven't seen that show, but I bet Elphaba would give Glinda another chance."

"None of that has anything to do with you. You're a liar."

"Yeah? Well, you're not perfect either. But you were still my friend."

"But I didn't lie to you. That's the difference."

"I'm sorry, Toni. So sorry. I wish I could take it back. Please give me another chance." I feel silly for begging but decide it's worth it.

She shifts her weight from one foot to the other. "I don't know, Connors. I just don't know."

"What don't you know?" I ask.

She shakes her head. "I have to go," she says, leaving me standing alone, wondering how I can keep messing things up as much as I do.

CHAPTER 30

Sunk by the Bell

The next morning, I come downstairs. I like these early mornings when the boys are all sleeping.

I smell cake. Real, honest-to-goodness cake. Mrs. Murphy is covering yellow cupcakes with homemade chocolate frosting. A good, thick layer of it. I can't wait to have one. I hop up to the counter.

She holds up a wooden spoon. "Forget it. I'll tell you the same thing that I'll tell the rest of 'em. These are for Adam's class today. There are twenty-four children in the class, so no, I can't spare just one."

"Do you really think that a wooden spoon can keep me from two dozen cupcakes? Didn't Family Services warn you of my violent tendencies?"

She seems to consider this, shaking her head in light disapproval, and I wish I hadn't said it, especially since Mrs. MacAvoy could be ringing the doorbell at any moment.

"What?" I ask. "I was just kidding about the violent tendencies thing."

"I don't like it when you describe yourself in a negative light. I don't like to hear you say bad things about yourself. Even if you're kidding."

God love the woman, but she's just a bit over the edge. "I tell you what. I'll tell you how beautiful I am if you give me a cupcake."

She holds up her deadly wooden spoon again. "Carley Connors. You really *are* beautiful. But beautiful or not, there will be no cupcakes for you or the rest of 'em."

She thinks I'm beautiful?

She goes back to frosting. "So, did you get a chance to talk to Toni?" she asks.

"Yeah, but it didn't go that well."

"Sometimes people need some time. That's all. It will be okay."

I hope she's right.

The doorbell rings. She goes to answer it while I plot how to steal some frosting.

I hear Mrs. Murphy's happy voice. "Oh, Mrs. MacAvoy. Please come in."

Oh no.

"I'm sorry to be so early, but I added this to an already insane schedule."

"Oh, is there news?"

There's a pause. "Not that I've heard. I just need to make sure Carley's okay."

"Carley?" Mrs. Murphy calls me like she's confused.

I appear in the foyer.

Mrs. MacAvoy's eyebrows jump. "Well, you look okay. Better than okay, actually."

"Is this something Family Services does routinely?" Mrs. Murphy asks.

"Oh no. Actually, Carley called me, expressing an interest in leaving."

"Carley?" The pain in Mrs. Murphy's tone rips into me. "Is that true?"

I look at the floor.

Mrs. Murphy stumbles over her words. "Are you? Are you here, then . . . to take her *away* from us?"

Take her away from us?

"No, I'm here to see if she's doing okay. Make sure she's in safe hands."

What have I done? I never thought of it like this. Well, I did . . . but I guess I didn't. I look up and Mrs. Murphy stares at me with such sad eyes and I wish that she were just mad at me. Mad is so much easier than this.

"Carley?" Mrs. Murphy asks me. "Do you want to leave? If you do, you're free to go any . . ."

"No! No!" I burst. "Don't make me go! I'm sorry. I don't know why I called. I just . . . I made a mistake. I don't want to go. Please don't make me go!"

"Well, normally I would take a look around," Mrs. MacAvoy says. "But I have a feeling things are well in hand."

"Yes, they are," Mrs. Murphy says, glancing at me. "I'm sorry that you had to come all this way for nothing."

Mrs. MacAvoy leaves with a softer face than I've seen before. I am such a jerk.

After she leaves, Mrs. Murphy turns to me and shakes her head. "I just don't get it. I don't understand, Carley."

I want to cry, but my body won't let me. "I just . . . it's just that . . ." I can't look at her anymore. "I don't belong here. I'm not one of you and this whole thing is . . . it's all just too . . . just too nice."

"You mean you don't want it to be nice here?"

"Well, not like that. No. It's just too nice . . . for me, I guess."

I glance only long enough to see confusion. "Carley? Are you saying that you don't belong here because it's too nice? You asked to leave because we're too *good* to you?"

Yeah, maybe that *was* it. I think it was. I nod.

"Oh, Carley. How can that be?"

"I hate it."

Her eyes widen. "You hate it that we're good to you?"

"No. Well, I guess . . ." My voice drops. "I hate it . . . that I don't hate it . . . that you're good to me."

Her fingertips touch her lips, and her eyes fill with water. I just want to crawl out of my skin. "My God, Carley" is all she says for a long time. I stay, though. I guess I trust her enough to want to know what she'll say.

"You deserve everything good the world has to offer. You deserve a family that loves you and cares for you."

One . . . two . . . three . . . four . . .

She touches my arm, which yanks me back.

She continues. "Carley, look at the person you are! It's phenomenal the strength you have." She brings her hand to her forehead. "It just isn't fair. But I know. I truly know . . ."

Sixteen . . . seventeen . . . eighteen . . .

"Carley?"

"Huh?"

"You deserve what we have to offer and more." Her voice cracks again. "And so much more."

I stiffen. "How can you say those things?" I yell. "You don't *know* those things!" I step away. The pain in my throat and the wetness in my eyes scare me. I don't know why bad things make me stronger and nice things make me weak.

"I *do* know, Carley. I've lived with you for six weeks now. I watch you with my boys and the sweet things you do for me. Don't you think that I've been paying attention? Give me a little credit." She tips her head and smiles a sad smile.

And that's the thing. Most of the time, it wasn't like my mother told me I was anything—good or bad. But when Mrs. Murphy tells me I'm smart, I am. When she tells me I'm funny, I am. When she tells me how thoughtful I am, I become that way. I swear, if she told me I was a duck, I'd be checking in my high tops for webbed feet.

"Carley," she says. I wonder why she always says my name.

"You're so strong. Strong enough to hide all this pain that you hold on to." She takes a breath. "But I think it's time to let it go."

"It's weak to cry. It's for suckers."

"Oh, Carley. It isn't weak, honey. It's human."

My insides swirl as I try to deny my body its right to tears. I begin to tremble but fold my arms and stiffen my back, trying to keep it away.

I count the spindles on the staircase, but it doesn't seem to be helping this time. "I have to go."

"Oh, Carley. You don't have to do this."

I hesitate, my feet wanting to run and my head wanting to wait.

"Stay with me," she says.

Spinning away, I run, making thirteen stairs in only six steps.

I go into the bathroom and turn on the water. I put my finger in the stream and watch as the stream becomes two. I count the splashes that land around the bowl of the sink. I close my eyes against the bright lights, willing my body to calm down. The swirling settles into my stomach with a thud.

I wish I could feel like I matter to someone for real. I just want a place to belong. But I'm so different from the Murphys. From everyone here.

And then something tells me—a part of me I don't hear much—*maybe you're not.*

CHAPTER 31

If You're Going to Lie to Yourself, Be Convincing

Daniel and I stand in the driveway again. Daniel stands with his arms folded, as usual, like he won't listen to a thing I say.

"Okay. I've been thinking," I say, spinning the basketball on my pointer finger.

"Is that why that stuff is oozing out of your ears?"

"Funny."

Who knew the kid had so much personality besides mama's boy extraordinaire. Still, I can't help thinking of the story he told me about his dad and the baseball stuff. "You know, you actually have talent," I lie.

"For what?" he asks.

"Basketball, idiot." I give him a shove—an experiment to see how he'll react. He takes it okay. "But you have one major set-back. I know what it is, but you won't like it."

"That I can't get the ball through the net?"

"No, no. That's going to work out great." I lean toward him. "For the *other* . . . *team!*" I laugh and dribble the ball through my legs.

"No, seriously." I hold the ball and look at him. "You're afraid."

"I am not! Afraid of what?"

"Afraid of the ball. The players. Taking chances."

He doesn't say anything.

"Look," I say, "my old coach used to say that forty percent of success in basketball is desire and another forty percent is confidence. You have the desire but no confidence."

"What's the other twenty percent?" he asks.

"Paying off the refs," I say, deadpan.

"Really?"

I dribble the ball and smile. "You're so gullible. Do you believe everything people tell you, Murphy?"

"Fine."

"Now, don't get all wound up again. I'm trying to help you, remember? Besides, we basketball morons have to stick together." I smile, hoping this will make him laugh.

"I still don't think I'm afraid."

"Then why do you act like you are?"

"Like when?" he asks, stepping back.

"Like when you have a perfect shot but you pass it instead of taking a shot yourself. Or someone is coming by you with the ball and you let him go right by."

"I guess."

"Do you know what courage is?"

"Give me a break. Listening to you?" He folds his arms.

"No, that would be dumb." I wink even though it feels unnatural. "Tell me what it is."

"Not being afraid of something."

"No! It's being afraid and doing it anyway. Like when your father runs into a burning building to save people. I'm sure he's afraid, but he does it anyway."

"Maybe you should run into a burning building." He smiles, and I wonder if I don't actually like him a little.

"After you make the Celtics. My life can't be spared until then."

"I'll work extra hard then," he says.

I laugh, and as I hear him join me, I bend over to rest my hands on my knees. "I wish I'd known earlier that you were so funny."

"Maybe you would have noticed if you weren't being a jerk all the time," Daniel says.

"Me? You were being a jerk, too."

"Why wouldn't I be mad?" He dribbles the ball. "Like the night you ran out of the house."

I stand. "Oh yeah." It feels like such a long time ago now. The night I ran to the orchard. "That was a lousy night."

"You can say that again."

"That was a lousy night?"

He ignores me. "My mother was wicked mad at *me* because *you* left. She wouldn't stop crying about you until my father finally came home and she could go look for you. I couldn't

142

understand why she flipped out so much. She said I was acting selfish. She's *never* said that to me before." He looks over at me and then away. "I guess I still don't get it sometimes."

"Your mother has been nice to me . . . but she'll never be my mom."

He nods again.

"So, Dan the Man . . ."

He half smiles.

"Another thing. You have to walk onto the court like you can do anything—even if you know you can't."

"What's the point of lying to myself?"

"Something about it." I shrug. "It works. Besides, if you put off vibes that you can handle yourself, other people will start treating you that way. Everything is attitude. I learned that at home." I guess I did learn some good things from my mother.

He looks surprised. "You never talk about your home."

"Yeah, well . . ."

"How come?"

"Let's just say, Daniel, that you're pretty lucky." Then I take a big chance and tell him, "I'd do anything for a family like yours."

Again he nods but doesn't say anything. I don't give him the chance to, though, as I throw the ball at him and he catches it. "Okay, Murphy. You drive to the basket and see if you can get by me."

"I'm gonna kick your butt!" he says.

"See? You're lying to yourself already!"

CHAPTER 32

Reservations for One

At lunch, I head across the cafeteria with my tray, thinking about how I've had to sit alone for eight days. I miss Toni. I sit at a table near the thin row of windows, along the curved wall. I move the carrots around my plate, and as I do, a carrot hits me in the chest. Just what I need.

Stellar. Throw food at the noob who's already sitting alone.

I look up. Rainer is at the next table; I have a feeling it's time to pay for what I did at the restaurant.

He smiles. "Find your mother yet? Might check under a rock." He laughs before lobbing another carrot at me. Normally, I'd stand up and tell him off. But I don't even care. About anything. I just want to walk out the front door of this school and keep walking and walking.

Another carrot hits me in the face.

"Is your brain any bigger than that carrot, Rainer?" Toni asks, dropping a tray on my table. "Do I need to teach you another lesson?"

"In your dreams," Rainer says.

Toni's loud laugh gets the attention of everyone nearby. "Oh my God. That comeback," she says, putting her hands over her heart. "You're brilliant."

He looks at me but talks to her. "So why don't we send the orphan back to where she came from? Don't they have homes for kids like that? Like the pound for dogs." Holding eye contact with me, he pretends to pant like a dog.

Toni laughs. "So you *do* want to fight me then. Huh, Rain Cloud?"

"I'd toast you, and you know it. We're not kids anymore."

Then she gets serious and leans toward him. "Look, you waste. I don't know who would win, but I promise you that I'd bloody you enough to make you the laughingstock of Smith Middle School."

He sits up straighter. "You think so, huh?"

Toni shakes her head in disgust. "Even though you'd need a magnifying glass to see your reputation, you wouldn't really want to mess with it, would you?"

Rainer shifts his weight, trying to decide what to do as Toni glares at him. He finally turns away. With a smirk, Toni sits across from me.

"What's with these carrots?" she asks. "Can't blame Rain Storm for chucking them, really. I'd sooner swallow live locusts than eat these."

"Thanks," I manage to say. "Thanks for helping me out."

"Did you ever think that maybe I just wanted a clean table so I could eat my lunch?" She smiles a crooked smile. "You know . . . it's not all about you, Connors."

I want to say more, but as Toni Byars moves on to complaining about Ruben's next project, I know that we're okay.

CHAPTER 33

Out on a Limb

I have been with the Murphys for forty-six days. The spring weather is finally here for good, and the trees are filled with leaves and everything's blooming. It would be a hundred degrees in Vegas now. I like it here.

Daniel and I are shooting hoops when the peace is broken by familiar yelling. Three houses down we see the younger Murphy boys with a kid wearing overalls. Michael Eric is holding his stomach and crying.

Daniel and I race down the street.

"Touch my brother again," Daniel threatens, "and I'll knock you into next week."

The overalls kid steps up. "Michael Eric is a baby. He needs his big *bwother* to help him," he says in a baby voice.

Michael Eric hugs my leg and I place my hand on top of his head, rubbing his hair.

"Who's this?" the kid asks, like I'm something he found on the bottom of his shoe.

"No," I say. "Who are *you*? The neighborhood farmer? Aren't you a little old for overalls?" I step up to him. He looks about nine years old but skinny enough for a stiff breeze to carry him away.

Michael Eric speaks through tears. "That's Jimmy Partin. He hits me and calls me a baby. He's a jerk face."

"He must be," I say, stepping up to him.

I must look like I'm going to whack him, because Daniel says, "Carley, you can't hit him. Mom will *kill* us if we hit first."

"Well, it seems like he *did* hit first," I say, looking at Michael Eric. "Besides, I'm willing to hit him and lie about it." The kid looks nervous, and I have to say I enjoy watching him squirm. "Just kidding," I say, pushing his shoulder with one finger. "You're too young for me to turn into a pancake." I take Michael Eric's hand. "Let's go back to the house."

As we turn to go, the twerp says, "You must be a Murphy. All they ever do is turn and run."

Now, this is the nicest thing anyone's said to me in a while, but I don't want the boys to see me run from this little creep. I decide to take the consequences for teaching him a lesson. I turn around. It must be in my eyes, because he runs.

"Who's running now?" I ask, snagging him easily.

"Carley, don't . . ." Daniel begins.

"Relax," I say. "Me and Jimmy here are going to be friends." I hold the straps of his overalls as he tries to twist away.

"You wouldn't dare hit me," he says, trying to look tough.

"You're right. I wouldn't. But I have something better." I drag him by the straps of his overalls to a tree that's in the side yard. It has nice climbing branches; I find a short, solid one.

I hoist Jimmy into the air and hang him by the straps of his overalls. He dangles there like a Christmas ornament. He kicks and yells. I lean in. "Touch a Murphy again—or tell anyone I did this—and I'll hang you from the gutters next time." I lean in closer. "I *mean* it."

Adam and Michael Eric run back to their house. I follow, Daniel walking beside me. We both look back to see Jimmy squirm and wiggle. He kicks his feet and turns apple red. He waves an angry fist as he tries to twist himself off of the branch. I wonder what the chances are that he'll keep quiet. Probably not good, but the words *a family sticks together* ring in my head.

Daniel shoves me and starts cracking up. "God, that was sweet to watch. But if my mom finds out, you're gonna really catch it, ya know."

"For Michael Eric?" I say without thinking. "I don't care what trouble I get in."

Daniel looks up. "I know you don't. That's what made it so great."

Then he shoves me again. And I shove him. And we laugh as we walk through two more of the neighbors' yards and, I have to admit, it feels pretty good.

When we get back to the Murphys', Michael Eric flashes his crooked baby teeth and throws up his arms. "Carley! You're my hero!" He leaps.

In my guts, I leap too.

If there's any punishment for making Jimmy into a Christmas ornament, it will be completely and totally worth it.

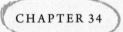

CHAPTER 34

Defying Gravity

Today Toni arrives while I'm sitting on the kitchen counter, "helping" with dinner.

"Hello, Toni. Good to see you again." Mrs. Murphy smiles at her and Toni kind of smiles back.

"Hey, Connors," Toni says. She motions to Mr. Murphy. "So, does he ever eat . . . or go to the bathroom . . . or do anything but watch the Sox?"

"Well, he puts out fires," I say, jumping down from the counter. "That's pretty good."

"Putting out fires, huh? Like the Sox going up in flames in the bottom of the ninth. An ocean couldn't put out that fire!"

"I heard that!" Mr. Murphy yells from the family room.

Mrs. Murphy chuckles. "Oh boy. Here they go."

"I thought I told you, Carley, that she isn't allowed over here!" he yells.

I know he's kidding, but still he makes me nervous.

Toni walks over. "Well, I could wait eighty-six years to come back. Because that's a really, really, really long time. Don't you think?"

"It wouldn't be long enough," he says.

They both laugh, and I think how funny it is that they are so alike.

"In fact, I was thinking," she adds. "Have you ever considered that it was Murphy's Law that the Sox couldn't come through all that time? I mean, does Red Sox Nation know it was your fault?"

"Toni, can you tell me how it came to be that you actually root for those blowhard Yankees?"

Toni's face darkens a little. "My dad loves the Yanks. He and my mom grew up in Jersey and . . . Well, it gives me a reason to e-mail him every day." She reaches into her back pocket and pulls out a folded piece of paper. "I print and carry his note with me the next day." She shuffles her feet a bit. "He doesn't usually answer . . ." She brightens. "But sometimes he does!"

Mrs. Murphy has stopped and turned to look at Toni, but I'd never stopped staring. Toni glances back at me, seeming embarrassed and much younger and not so tough.

"That's cool, Toni," I say. "You're lucky to have notes from your dad. I've never met my father." I hope it makes her feel better to have a little of her dad rather than none.

Mr. Murphy stares too. He presses his lips together before patting the couch next to him. "C'mon in here, Toni." Then he yells, "You too, Carley! Come on in here and see your beloved Ellsbury!"

I'm surprised that she heads right over. So do I.

"Ellsbury, Connors?" Toni asks. "Are you serious?"

"Who do you like?" I ask. "A-Roid?"

"Ha!" Mr. Murphy says. He ruffles my hair and says, "That's my girl!"

And I really do wish I were.

In the fireman room, Toni lounges on the bed as we listen to her *Wicked* CD. A song called "What Is This Feeling?", also known as the "loathing song," comes on and she cracks up. "Remember, Connors, how we couldn't stand each other?"

"Wait a minute," I tease. "You didn't like me?"

"I liked you like poison ivy." She laughs again and throws a fire truck pillow in my direction. Then she takes a deep breath. "So, Connors." She looks serious. "What's the deal with this foster kid thing? Did your mother die or something?"

"No," I say, shifting my weight.

"Did she leave you in a basket on some church steps or what?"

"No," I snap.

"You don't have to tell me if you don't want to, Connors, but I've been wondering." She picks at her sneaker. "You know, wondering how bad it was. Kids don't end up in foster care for paper cuts."

I can tell it's not just curiosity. I can tell it worries her. I look out the window. "Let's just say that my mother cared more about her new husband than she did about me."

"So she left with him?"

"Not exactly," I mumble.

"It was bad, wasn't it, Connors?" I can tell she's praying for a particular answer—one she knows she won't get.

I nod.

"That's why you were in the hospital? Because of them?"

"Yeah."

She sits up fast. "You know, I'm pretty ticked that they would hurt you," she says. "If I'm around and they try to do something like that, I'll hit them so hard they'll have to carry their teeth in a baggie."

I laugh.

"Not funny, Connors. Believe it."

"Sounds like something you'd say to Rainer."

Now she's laughing. "Yeah, it does. I'll have to use it on him." She turns to me. "Did you know he used to carry dental floss to school every day?"

"No way!"

"Yes! All through the third and fourth grade."

"Why?"

"Because he's Rainer, that's why!" She jumps. "Oh, by the way, he was acting weird yesterday. He actually came over and didn't act like a simp."

"What's the story? Is he delirious?" I ask.

"Our little boy is growing up," she says, sniffing.

She falls back on the bed, and all is quiet for a while. "So," I begin. "You like your dad, huh?"

She looks surprised. "Yeah. I like my dad a lot. His only fault is that he's invisible. He says he works those hours in Japan to give us a good life, but I'd take a smaller house with him home in a heartbeat."

"I wish my mother was different too, you know?" I confess to Toni. "Before coming here, I didn't even know I wanted her to be different. It's like when Mrs. Murphy kept trying to get me to try Hawaiian pizza. I thought it sounded gross. But I finally tried it, and I love it. I guess sometimes you don't know what you want because you don't know it exists."

"So what *is* your mom like?" she asks.

"Well, if you found the person most unlike your mother on the planet, it would be my mother. For one, we'd shop for clothes in the Salvation Army drop boxes."

She sits up quick. "No way! Really? You mean the metal boxes? Not the store?"

"Yup. You got it. Under dark of night with flashlights."

"We have to try that, Connors. That sounds like the best!"

"Oh, yeah. It was the best all right." I don't want to keep talking about my mother. I throw the pillow back at her.

The first few notes of "Defying Gravity" play. Toni stands on my bed and does the intro perfectly. I jump up and join her and say Elphaba's part. Once the real song starts, we both sing everything, and I pay more attention to the words than I ever have. And as I listen, I realize that Toni and I feel the same way about things.

That we've both changed. That we're tired of having the world push us into places we don't want to be. That we're both scared of losing love that maybe we never had to begin with. That we can have whatever we want in our lives; it's only a matter of deciding. But Toni and I don't have to do it alone. We have each other.

CHAPTER 35

Order on the Court!

Carley," Mrs. Murphy says. "Daniel has a game tonight. It would be nice if you would go."

I bite into a saltine. "Sure. Sounds good." A few weeks ago, it would've been more likely that I'd run off and join the Russian army than find myself actually liking Daniel. But I do.

So when I sit down on the bleacher next to Mrs. Murphy, I haven't brought a notebook or anything to read.

Before the game I grab him by the shoulders and shake him. "All right, Murphy. You go kick some you know what. Remember. Dribble low to the floor and protect that ball. Protect it. Don't forget that arc on your shot. Okay?"

"Got it."

"Take a shot if you've got it!" I yell. "You are invincible! Remember that!"

Mrs. Murphy stares at me.

"What?" I say, turning. "Is something wrong?"

She sputters. "Are you *kidding* me? No, I just can't believe it! I couldn't be happier!"

I turn in time to see Daniel take a shot that almost goes in but rolls out.

He looks nervous.

"That's okay, Daniel! Keep at it!"

Daniel makes a decent pass and later makes a good bounce pass to another player, who goes in for a layup. He pumps his fist and looks at us.

Then, unbelievably, Daniel makes a basket. I'm on my feet and Mrs. Murphy looks back and forth between Daniel and me. The rest of the team is already running back up the court as he stands there with a smile that covers his whole face.

His coach yells, "Daniel! Keep it moving! Down on D!"

He wakes up and follows his team. Within about four minutes, he dribbles the ball down the court and shoots for another basket, which misses. I clap. "That's okay, Daniel! Way to take the shot!"

Daniel is taken out for a while, but we make eye contact while he's on the bench. His coach ruffles his hair, and he smiles. I give him a nod and a thumbs-up, because I remember how my coach did that for me. When Daniel goes back in, he takes a shot from beyond the arc, and I swear I stopped breathing as it sailed up.

Swish!

I'm on my feet, yelling, "Dan the Man!" His mother claps like the kid just won the lottery. Even Adam and Michael Eric pull their heads out of their Matchboxes game to look. Two of

Daniel's teammates high-five him; the kid is happier than I've ever seen him.

Daniel only makes the two baskets, but he earns some respect from the other players, which feels as good as the points do. I remember.

At the end of the game, Mrs. Murphy squeezes my arm. "I don't know what you did, but thank you, Carley. It's such a relief to see him happy and having fun." She shakes her head as her gaze wanders back to the court. "All these gifts you have, Carley. All these gifts you have."

CHAPTER 36

Late-Night Surprise

On my fifty-second night, I wake up to Elvis Presley music. After lying there for a while, I have to go see where it's coming from.

At the bottom of the stairs, I recognize the song as "Can't Help Falling in Love." Any self-respecting Las Vegas resident can sing any Elvis song there is. This one, though, isn't like the others. It's actually kind of nice.

I sneak through the dining room and lay my hand on the door frame leading into the kitchen. I lean in, listening.

Mr. and Mrs. Murphy are dancing.

She rests her head on his chest with her arms around his waist. His cheek rests on the top of her head. They move as one, back and forth and around.

I've seen my mother dance with plenty of guys, and it's always grossed me out. But this? This is like a real love story come to life. I mean, they're just dancing, but I can feel it. And everything else I see during the day makes sense. The way he puts his hand on her waist as he reaches around her to get a glass from the cabinet. The way they look at each other and laugh when the rest of us are wondering what's so funny. The way he winks at her across the dinner table.

What would it be like to love someone like that? Does my mother know what that's like? Will I?

I don't watch for long, because I feel like some sort of weird stalker. As I head back upstairs, though, I feel lucky that I got to see it.

CHAPTER 37

Sinking Feelings and Other Plumbing Problems

Mrs. Murphy comes in my room and closes the door as if it could break and sits on the bed. "I have some news for you."

I take a deep breath and hold it.

"Um . . ." Mrs. Murphy speaks carefully. "I spoke with Mrs. MacAvoy. There's some good news for you, Carley!" She's sitting up extra straight, and she bites her lip a little; she isn't happy at all—just trying to make me think she is. "It turns out that your mother is doing much better. In fact, she's going to be transferred to a rehab facility."

"Rehab? For drugs?" I gasp.

"No, no. Physical rehab. She needs some help overcoming her injuries. They'll teach her to walk again."

"My mother can't *walk*?" I do not react. On the outside, anyway.

"She will, but she needs some time. And . . . well, apparently she wants to see you."

I've waited for this for such a long time, but now that it's here, I don't know if I want to go see her or not. "That's great," I say, trying to smile since we're both faking here.

"So, we'll give her some time to settle in, and then we'll visit her. How would that be?"

How would that be? She asks like she wants to know if I want rainbow sprinkles on my ice cream cone. "Okay," I say. "What are we having for dinner?"

"Oh. That chicken casserole I do."

"Ooh. The one with the stuffing. That's wicked good." I actually feel a little better.

"Yeah. It is. I mean, I'm glad you like it." I can see her studying me—trying to figure out what's really going on.

"Mrs. Murphy?"

"Yeah?"

"Is my mother going to prison? Remember that policeman who was here? He said my mother was in trouble."

"No, Carley, she's not in trouble. I was going to talk to you about that. It seems the charges against your mother have been dropped in exchange for her testimony." She leans forward. "Do you know what that means?"

I nod. So she's going to rat on Dennis. I don't mind if that jerk goes to prison. I don't want my mother to go to prison, but I'm not in a rush to get back to her either.

"One more thing," she says.

I'm both eager and terrified to hear this.

She holds out a piece of paper. "I have the phone number to her room in case you want to call her."

I wonder what she would say to me if I called. That she's done with me? I want to take the paper so badly, but I can't move. Like if I took it, it would burn my fingers.

Mrs. Murphy finally puts the number on the nightstand and leaves.

Later that night, I dial my mother's phone number from the Murphys' bedroom. The phone rings and I'm not sure what I'll do when she answers. It rings five times and just as I move to hang up, her voice is there. Raspy and tired, but unmistakably her. "Hello?"

I count the pictures on the wall.

"Hello?" she asks again.

I should say something, but what? That I'm sorry? That I love her? Or that I'm not sure if I'm sorry? Or I'm not sure that I love her?

"Carley? Is that you?" she asks, and I feel my body jolt like when I got the shock from plugging in our fan when I was little.

"Yeah?" I hold my breath.

"My *God*. They told me they put you in some foster care place. Are you okay?"

That's ironic. "Yeah."

"We'll be together soon, Carley. I promise."

I feel like the things I should say are the things I can't say. And the things I could say are the things I shouldn't say.

"Carley?"

"Yeah."

"My girl is not usually at a loss for words."

My girl? "Yeah."

I hang up the phone. I don't say good-bye or anything because I want her to wonder what I might have said. Or maybe that's just me who would spend all that time wondering.

When You Care Enough to Send the Very Worst

Mrs. Murphy's back is to me as she makes me a sandwich for school. When she turns to hand me the brown bag with my lunch, I sense trouble in her face. She lays a five-dollar bill in front of me; you'd think I would be happy, but I know better.

"Carley," she begins. "Mother's Day is coming up. And I'm not saying that you *have* to get or even that you *should* get a card for your mother, but I wanted you to have the money just in case you choose to."

My mother. I probably should send her something, I guess. I hate the thought of it, though—some sappy, sweet card for her?

Then I look at Mrs. Murphy and wonder if I am supposed to get her a card. I wonder if Hallmark makes a "Happy Mother's Day to someone who isn't the slightest bit related to me and only took me in because I'm pathetic but what the heck, the state throws in a little money—which isn't worth it, I'm sure" card.

I realize that I've been staring at her. And she stares back. I slide the bill off the counter like a poker player takes his hand. I fold it up until it can't be folded any more and push it down into my jeans pocket with my thumb. I realize that I've not said thank you or good-bye or *anything* until I am in the driveway. I turn around and she's there, in the dining room window. Her right hand waves like she's playing the piano, and she looks sad. I wave back and leave.

I swing the door of the Hallmark store open too hard and it bangs. Toni follows.

The first thing I see are a bunch of signs on the wall for sale. They all say BELIEVE. The first thing I notice is that right smack in the middle of the word is "lie." It figures. Besides, what am I supposed to believe in anyway?

"A pink nightmare," I mumble, walking toward the Mother's Day display.

Toni elbows me. "Have you ever noticed that the bigger the L-word, the uglier the card?"

She's holding a card with LOVE written in giant letters. I remember the day I told my mother that *love* spelled backward is the first four letters in "evolve." She said it figured since you have to change for anyone to really love you. I think back to that now as I watch Toni brush off her cool New York jacket, wondering if it's the truth.

I reach for a card. It stabs. MOM, WHAT WOULD I EVER DO WITHOUT YOU?

I read it over and over. Eight words. Ten syllables.

Toni touches me and I jump. "Jumpy, Connors? What gives?"

"I don't want to give my mother a card."

"Look, Connors. You've never told me in detail why you landed at the Murphys, but I'm going to assume that she doesn't deserve a Mother's Day card. Skip it if it winds you up."

"But I feel like I should. I'm still her daughter."

Toni shrugs. "Well, look at it this way, Connors. It's only a card. It's not like you're gonna sit down and write a poem for her or tattoo 'Mom' on your arm. Some dork probably wrote these. Some dork who wears suspenders and lives in his mother's basement. So just let the dork do the talking, and you're off the hook."

I nod, thinking about how much I would miss Toni if I ever have to leave. I grab a card quickly. "Oh my God. Look at this one. Warm and tender?"

"Sounds like fried chicken," Toni says, leaning in.

"It does!" I say. "They should have a rotisserie chicken in an apron."

"Pulling a roast out of the oven," Toni adds. "The chicken would probably make beef, don't you think?"

"Or it could pull out another chicken with a suicide note stuck to it." I'm laughing. Laughing really hard, but it scares me, like I'm walking a fence between laughing hard and crying.

Toni is talking, but I can't listen. There isn't enough air in the store. These cards are a slap in the face, listing all of the things that real mothers do. Knowing that I have a mother who does so little of it. It's not like I'd expect her to stay home at night or join the PTA. I mean, all I want her to do is look at me the way Mrs. Murphy looks at her kids. Like I'm the best thing ever. Like she loves me more than anyone else.

I reach for a card, and I decide to buy it no matter what it says. "C'mon. Let's go."

Toni grabs it and reads it on the way to the register. "Hey, nice card, Connors."

Late that night, I sit under the hero sign. I open the card. I wipe my palms on my jeans. I worry Mrs. Murphy will walk in on me, but Jay Leno is on, so I know the house would have to be on fire for her to leave *that*. I read the card: THANKS FOR ALL THE REALLY BIG THINGS YOU DO, BUT ALSO FOR THE 45 BILLION LITTLE THINGS. BET YOU DIDN'T KNOW I WAS COUNTING. I add, "Ha-ha," and then sign, "Love, Carley Connors."

I sure hope Mrs. Murphy likes it.

CHAPTER 39

Summon the Book Eater

Since I read those cards at the store yesterday, I realize how Mrs. Murphy is like a lot of them. Kind of too good to be true, maybe. I remember she's human when I hear her puking in the bathroom.

Adam and Michael Eric are outside the door and they are freaked.

I hear her retch. Then she says, "Mommy's okay, guys. Why don't you . . ." And then she retches again.

"Hey, guys," I say. "I think your mom wants to be alone. She sounds a little sick."

Michael Eric looks up at me with a milky face. "But she sits with *me* when I throw up."

"Well," I say, thinking about how lucky he is, "grown-ups tend to do that alone." I squat. "Hey! I have an idea! Would you like to see my secret reading cave?"

Their eyes widen.

"Get some books and we'll find the secret reading cave and I'll read to you." They run off. I knock softly on the door. "Mrs. Murphy, I'll read to the boys. You can sleep for a while. I can make dinner and put them to bed and stuff, okay?"

There's a really long silence. In fact, I worry that she's fallen in or something. Finally, I hear a raspy, "Thank you, Carley. I think that might be good."

I grab a flashlight out of the garage and meet the boys in the family room. "Follow me," I say. I put my pointer finger over my mouth. "Be very quiet. The Book Eaters may hear you. We must reach the magical secret reading cave before they see us and eat . . . our . . . books!"

"Wicked awesome!" Adam says.

"If I see a Book Eater, I'll kick his butt!" says Michael Eric.

Adam asks, "What do they look like?"

"Book Eaters?" I ask.

He nods.

"They're big and heavy like tanks—that color green too. Unless they stand in front of something, then they change like chameleons."

Adam smiles.

"That way they can hide. But when they smile, you can see their teeth. And they're usually chewing on pages. They devour books like you guys eat ice cream."

"Wow. That's fast," Adam says.

Michael Eric nods likes he's proud of how fast he eats.

"Here we are!" I say. "The secret reading cave!"

"The closet?" Adam asks.

"Not a *closet*. A secret reading cave—safe from the Book Eaters."

They scurry in, and we settle down on the floor of the cleanest closet I've ever seen. Any sound we make is shushed by Michael Eric, who is afraid of being found. I sit cross-legged while each of them leans on one of my legs. Michael Eric sits Mr. Longneck up to listen too. "Which book should we read first?" I ask. "You scare a Book Eater away by loving a book, so let's read a favorite one first."

Michael Eric grabs a bright green one. "This is Mommy's favorite."

Adam nods. "The tree and the boy book. Yup. She likes that one."

"*The Giving Tree*," I read aloud. It is about a tree and a boy. Simple enough. But every page annoys me more than the last. It's dumb. The tree in the book is so nice, no matter how much of a twit the boy is. Why would the tree do that? I finish it but am happy to get to a book about trucks that even the boys enjoy more. But I can't get that *Giving Tree* out of my head.

I wish the Book Eater would come by so I could slide it under the door.

CHAPTER 40

Ironing the Wrinkles In

When I wake up, I check on Mrs. Murphy. She's ironing. "Do you feel better?"

"I'm okay. I thought I'd get some of this done while the boys are still sleeping. Why are you up so early?"

I shrug.

"Can't sleep?"

I shrug again.

"I can't thank you enough for watching the boys last night. I don't know what I would have done if you hadn't been here."

I feel warmer.

She seems a little embarrassed. "You know, I'm not used to people taking care of *me*."

"Well," I say slowly, "I'd . . . I'd do anything for you, ya know."

She stops in midstroke and stands the iron up.

"I mean, I really would."

She tilts her head and stares, her mouth turned up on just one side. "Well . . . *that* may be the nicest thing I've heard in a long time. And listen, if I hadn't been throwing up all last night, I might have even hugged you for it! You're lucky," she says with a wink.

I try to decide if I'm disappointed or not.

She flips the shirt over and begins ironing again. "So, to what do I owe the pleasure of your company? Did you need something?"

I don't answer at first. I stare at the iron as it slowly moves over the wrinkles in the shirt. I am mesmerized by the little puffs of steam that rise out of the iron as she gently pushes all the wrinkles out. That's what Mrs. Murphy does.

I point at the shirt. "Have you noticed that all of your clothes are happy? Like, you never wear tan or black. Always bright stripes and stuff."

"Bright colors keep me awake."

I'm too nervous to laugh. "Can I ask a favor?"

She looks serious all of a sudden. "Of course."

"Well, I . . . it's just that . . ."

"Yes?" Her slow tone is like a rope that pulls the words from me, even though I don't want to let them go.

"I wanted to ask you a question." I force myself to look her in the face as I ask. It's always a person's very first reaction that you need to watch for. "Well, I was wondering if . . . you would mind if . . . I mean if it's okay that . . ."

She laughs. "C'mon, spit it out!"

"If I can call you *Mom*."

Her smile fades and is replaced with worry. "Oh, Carley, I just—"

I interrupt. "Oh, I know that it's pretend and it's only for a little while—you know, until I have to go—but it just seems like it would be easier than calling you Mrs. Murphy because it's only a fourth of the syllables and, well, you kind of feel like a mother—well, a second mother, 'cause you know I have a mother of my own, but I just thought it would be nice until I go. Just until I go. I mean, I guess I am gonna go."

Her silence screams an answer. I feel like my head rests firmly in a guillotine. She reaches for me and I twist away.

"You and I have a very special relationship."

"But not special enough."

Her eyes brim with tears. "I just don't think it would be a healthy thing for you."

"It has nothing to do with me."

"It has everything to do with you."

I back up into the door frame.

She talks fast now. "I don't mean it like it sounded. I think it would be unfair to you. You have a mother—a very lucky one. Carley, I'd love to have been your mother."

I know this is supposed to be a nice thing, but it cuts so deep, leaves such a hole, I feel like I may turn inside out. I notice the patterns on her bedspread. I realize I'm counting out loud.

"Carley?"

Twenty-one, twenty-two, twenty-three. What a jerk I am. How could I be so dumb?

"Try to understand, Carley. You and I both know that you'll have to go someday and I just—"

I interrupt. "But what about that book? That book about adoption? I thought I was going to stay here." I spiral and she deflates.

"Oh, honey..."

I step back. Honey?

Her shoulders slump. "It just isn't in the cards. Your mother is doing better and better and Mrs. MacAvoy has said that the court will rule to grant her custody of you when she's ready."

How can I go back after what she did?

She steps toward me, and I step back into the door, putting my hands up in front of me, palms facing her. "When you do go, Carley, it will be excruciating"—she clears her throat—"for this family because, in many ways, you're one of us now. I think leaving would be harder for me *and* for you if you called me Mom. Not to mention..."

I can tell this is something I don't want to hear.

"...My boys."

I hate how she says "my."

"Carley, I..."

I cut her off. "Fine." I step back again. "Then I have just one more question."

"What's that?" Her voice cracks.

"Will you just leave me alone, then? Leave me alone until I leave."

I bolt before she can answer.

I want to hate her, but I can't.

I feel so sad I can hardly stomach it. Mrs. Murphy didn't mean to, but she's taught me what I'll never have. Brought me to the candy store and given me just a taste—just enough that I'll always know what I'm missing. And those kids—always watching them live here. The knowledge that I'm not loved like her kids are. Not by her and not by my own mother.

I have to remember.

I must.

Don't forget your place.

Don't forget who you really are.

CHAPTER 41

Mind Over Matter

The "can I call you *Mom*" execution was yesterday; it plays over and over in my head. Last night, I claimed sickness so I could skip helping with or eating dinner. Even when she resorted to making an apple pie, I refused. Killed me, but I did.

Before leaving for school today, I stuffed the Mother's Day card for Mrs. Murphy into my backpack. On the bus, I ripped it into pieces and then dropped a few pieces in the trash at the beginning of each class. It was my routine and about the only thing I thought of all day. I didn't want anyone piecing them together. Not even me.

I think that M-O-M must stand for "mind over matter"—like if I don't mind, it doesn't matter. Problem is, I do mind.

I know that Mrs. Murphy feels bad. The air is thick whenever we're in the same room, so I avoid her. I almost bump into her, though, as she comes out of her bedroom. "Oh, Carley!" she says like I haven't seen her for weeks. "How are you doing?" she asks.

"Okay," I say, turning to leave.

"You want to help me with dinner?" she asks, which is code for just hanging out.

"Naw. I'm gonna read."

"Sure you don't want to help? I would really like your company!"

"I have a lot to do."

"Okay then." She turns to go, takes two steps down the stairs, stops, and turns back around. "Carley, I'm just heartsick about what happened Sunday morning."

"I haven't even thought about it," I lie.

She comes back up two steps and her talking speeds up again. "What concerns me is that you know I wouldn't hurt you on purpose."

I turn to go.

"Carley. You know I wouldn't hurt you, right?"

"It doesn't matter," I say, because I don't want to talk about it. The part that keeps me safe would rather stay mad at her.

I hear her voice crack. I turn around, clutching my book, and am ready to tell her she cries *way* too much.

I open my mouth, but she interrupts me. "I love you, Carley. You know, I just *do*."

I turn away. That's the last thing I wanted to hear.

CHAPTER 42

Back Against the Wall

The tally on the back of the hero sign is sixty. It has already been a long day and it's only lunch. Mostly because it's Mother's Day.

Not like Mother's Day has ever been my favorite holiday, but this has to be the worst. I have to sit around while Mrs. Murphy reads cards from everyone else. I feel terrible that I tore up that Mother's Day card and don't have one to give her.

I wish more than anything that I had a mother I could give a sappy card to. That my mother could be my mother. Or that Mrs. Murphy wanted to be my mother. That anyone wanted to be my mother. A Labrador retriever maybe. Anyone.

Mrs. Murphy comes by my room after we've cleaned up. "Mind if I come in?"

I shrug.

She walks over and sits on the bed beside me. "Today is a tough day, huh?"

I shrug.

"You want to talk?"

"Nah. I'm fine." All I can hear are the things I can't say.

"Fine, huh?" she says. "You don't lie very well."

It's funny how she knows me. I so wish I had the card to give her now. She deserves a card from me.

"I'm just tired," I say, forcing myself to look her in the eye.

"Okay." She pauses. "Hey, listen, I have something to tell you." Uh-oh.

"Remember how I told you that your mom wants to see you, Carley? And that you would be going to visit her?"

"Do I have to go?" I blurt out.

She puts her hand on my back, and I am instantly on my feet. I am surprised at how quick my breathing is. "When?" I ask. "When do I have to go?"

"Tomorrow."

"Fine." I am so worried about how my mother will act toward me.

"Carley." Her tone reminds me of when she's talking to her boys. "It's been a tough day being Mother's Day, I know. And this visit is a difficult thing. No one would ever say you're not strong, but you know you don't have to be all the time."

My eyelids come down like window shades. I count my breaths.

"It's okay, Carley. Whatever it is, we can talk it out."

Her eyes are moist, and she looks like something hurts. I stare at her shoulder.

I know that if I tried to rest my head on her shoulder, it would be okay. But I know I can't. Hearing the boys laughing downstairs reminds me that she isn't mine.

Mrs. Murphy picks up a pen on the side table and plays with it. "Well, I've had an interesting day. I was in town with the boys."

I let my breath back out. Slowly.

"We were walking by a bench where an older lady was smoking a cigarette. Michael Eric looked up at me and said, 'Hey, Mom! Check out this fool smoking a cigarette!' And he was *loud*. And she was right there."

I crack up because I can see it so clearly in my head. God, I just love that kid.

Mrs. Murphy points at me. "Yeah, sure! Easy for you to laugh! I was horrified. She looked at me like I was the worst mother this side of the planet."

"Well, she must have been a fool then."

Her expression softens again, so I kill the moment quickly. "Hey! You were a teacher. I have a question. You know that book *The Giving Tree*?"

"Sure. I've read it to my classes and to all of my sons. Many times."

"Why would you want to teach anyone a lesson like that?"

"How do you mean?"

"Well, that you should just give people whatever they ask for and never expect anything in return? Like if a friend just kept coming and asking for stuff and never even said thank you. It just seems like a book about a selfish jerk and a sucker. Who'd have friends like that?"

"Well, Carley." I can see she measures her words. "That book is about unconditional love. You know, loving no matter what. Giving completely of yourself because it makes you happy to give, not because you expect anything in return. It's about loving someone more than yourself. And you'll notice that the tree doesn't mind."

"The tree is just dumb."

"Well, not really. But it isn't so much about friendship; I agree with you on that."

"What do you mean? You agree with me, but you don't agree with me? I don't get it."

"Carley, honey. It's about unconditional love." She hesitates before finishing. "*The Giving Tree* is about a mother's love for her child."

I step back against the wall again.

CHAPTER 43

Pals Spelled Backwards

My mother's room smells like a mixture of rubbing alcohol and floor cleaner. The walls have cheery yellow and blue stripes and, I guess, are supposed to convince you that you're happy to be here.

My mother's face is so white that it seems dusted with powdered sugar. It is also thin and, as I walk up to her bed, I am afraid to touch her. I bend over to see if her chest rises and falls with each breath. I open my mouth to say her name, but all I get is a squeak. She opens her eyes.

"Carley Cake," she whispers.

"Hi, Mom. How do you feel?" The irony of the question winds through my head.

She reaches out to me with an open hand. Just like she did that night. The night I thought she was reaching for help.

My chest aches when she begins to sing. Raspy. Slow.

> *"We're pals together*
> *Rootin' pals, tootin' pals*
> *Birds of a feather."*

I see the words as she sings them. I realize that *pals* spelled backward is *slap*.

"How's my girl?" she says with a voice that reminds me of Mrs. Murphy.

There's a feeling, deep down, that shoots up through the middle of me. I try to shove it down, but it wants to come no matter what I think of it. The way she talks all nice and calls me "Carley Cake." It *sounds* the way it should, but it doesn't *feel* the way it should.

I want to tell her never to call me that again. That she doesn't deserve it. But instead, I sit down, put my palms together and stuff them in between my knees. We're both quiet for a while. I can feel it. Two broken hearts and neither one knows how to fix anything.

She stares. I can't sit still.

"What?" I finally ask.

"You. You look so different. Your hair. It looks nice fixed that way. And those clothes. I hardly recognize you."

I know I look different. I feel different too.

"Do you remember the first day of kindergarten?" she asks me.

This catches me off guard.

"You were so cute that day, thinking you were all grown up. Your teacher had that wild red hair. Do you remember that?"

"Yeah," I say. "I liked her. She had a huge stash of Play-Doh."

"You told her that her hair was nutso but it looked good on her."

"*I* said that?"

"Yeah, you did. Full of fire from the very beginning."

I think she is describing herself more than me. I remember the end of that day—when my mother wasn't at the front of the apartment building to meet the bus, and they wouldn't let me get off. I had to ride the whole route back to the school, and then they couldn't get my mother to answer the phone. One of the secretaries stayed late.

"What are you thinking about?" she asks me.

"Kindergarten."

"What about it?"

"The secretary was nice."

"What about what you said to your third-grade teacher? Do you remember that?"

"Oh, how I said he looked like the butt of a wombat? Yeah, he didn't like that much." In the past, I would have laughed, and she would have told me more. Instead, I think how I probably wouldn't do that now. Make a teacher mad just to make my mother laugh.

"So, anyway . . . ," she says, "what's this couple like that have you? Are they being good to my baby girl? Do you like them?"

"Yeah, I really do. The mother is wicked nice."

My mother's eyes get squinty and I know this look. The clouds are rolling in. There's a storm coming. But she surprises me instead. She smiles in a way I haven't seen before. "But you're *my* Carley Cake, right?"

I think back to when I was. Then I remember Dennis. My mouth spits out, "Don't call me Carley Cake anymore."

Her smile fades. "I have the right to do anything I want. You are *my* daughter."

"Well, it would be nice if maybe you acted like I was."

"I've been plenty good to you. But sometimes you're just a brat who expects too much."

"Yeah. Like not landing in a hospital. Or a foster home? But that's all right—if this had never happened, I would never have known what I was missing."

"What do you mean? Missing what?"

"I know what a happy family is like now. I know what it's like not to worry all the time. And I don't shop for clothes in Dumpsters."

"Oh, so you're all high-class now? It's all about money?"

"No, it's not. It's about feeling like someone cares if I'm okay."

"Can you see me in this bed? Nothing like kicking a person when she's down."

"Better than holding a *foot*." As soon as it comes out, I wish I had not said this. "Sorry," I say, and I am. Yet I do want her to know that what she did was awful. I want her to know so much— that I love her anyway and hate her at the same time. I want her to know that I want to live with the Murphys forever, but that I'd die without her.

There's a lump in my throat.

She's angry. "You crying now, Carley? They turned you into a sucker, didn't they?"

I think about how Mrs. Murphy cries, and she's one of the strongest people I know.

There's a welling up inside of me like a glass that's filled too much. I have to ask. "Why did you do that? With Dennis, I mean. Why did you . . . hold me like that? Didn't you know what he would do?"

"No, I didn't. At first I was just thinking I'm his wife. I swore to be loyal, for better or worse. But I didn't know—"

"Are you *kidding* me?" I interrupt. "That's the best you can come up with?" I feel like I'm going to puke.

"Look, Carley. Life is complicated." She straightens the sheet across her lap. "But *fine*. I love you. Is that what you want to hear?"

"Heartwarming."

"Well, maybe instead of coming here to the hospital and upsetting me while I'm in pain, you could keep quiet long enough for me to explain what happened."

How I wish she could. But how could she possibly explain holding me down?

"Carley, when I met Dennis—"

I interrupt. Yelling. "No! I don't want to hear about Dennis or your dumb excuses! You *said* he would take care of us. You promised. You *said* he'd be my dad."

I step toward her, remembering the disappointment of finding out who he really was, and knowing she was going to marry him anyway. "I knew what he was like. I tried to tell you!"

"Carley, I don't have to answer to you. I'm the mother here. Besides, I tried to help you."

"Help me? Are you kidding?" My nails dig into my palms. "Do you know what a mother is?" I blurt out. "A mother is Julie Murphy. Her kids don't sleep in the bathtub when her friends are staying over for a party, and they're not the only kid who can't sign up for anything because they can't get a ride home. Julie Murphy is a better mother than you could ever hope . . ."

A shade comes down over my mother's face. "Visiting hours are over," she says coldly. "Why don't you run along with your . . . *new mother.*" She waves me out.

But I can't leave yet. I think of *The Little Mermaid.* I think of how my mother made mustaches for me out of whipped cream. How we'd eat frozen pizza and watch reruns. How, when I was much younger, she'd talk in funny cartoon voices when I was scared of the dark. I remember that in good times, she could make my stomach ache from laughing.

"I don't want a new mother," I say. "I just want you to . . ." I can't say any more. I want to ask why she didn't love me enough, but I'm afraid of her answer.

"Well, isn't it a shame that I'm just not good enough for you, Carley."

I'm angry and confused. I think only of running. So I do. I run. While my mother pounds in the final nail. "That family can *have* you!"

CHAPTER 44

Playing with Fire

Mr. Murphy sits on the couch watching the Red Sox, wearing his Dropkick Murphys T-shirt. I know that to disturb him in the eighth inning is a sin and I would, undoubtedly upon my death, be sent to that great dugout underground. But I probably have a ticket in that direction anyway.

"Mr. Murphy?" I ask.

"Yes, Carley?"

"Do you ever have to leave some people behind? You know, in a fire?"

His face darkens, and he glances back at the game. I know that I shouldn't have asked. But something inside me just has to know.

"One child, two women, one man."

"Huh?"

"That's who I've had to leave behind."

Four people. "Oh."

He nods slowly. "Yeah."

I feel courageous and continue. "Well, how do you decide? I mean, how do you decide who to save and who to leave?"

He glances at me but answers while watching the TV. "Well, Carley, I don't really decide. The fire does. She always wins when she wants to. The first rule is that your own safety is paramount. I try to remember that I'm no good to anyone dead."

"Do you think of your family when you're in a fire?"

"Will you get the pitcher out of there!" he yells at the TV. He looks at me. "You know, you'd think for eight million a year, he could throw a ball over a plate."

The doorbell rings, so I get up. I am almost out of the room when he says, "I don't think of the boys in the middle of a fire because I'm trying to save lives—including my own." He clears his throat. "But on every trip, you know, as we're on the engine going to the call, when I'm suited up and everything, I pull out a picture of Julie and the boys, and I remember why I need to come home."

I don't expect this answer that makes my stomach roll.

I hear Mrs. Murphy open the front door and Toni comes in. "Hey, Connors."

"Hey."

"The Red Sox again? You know," she says to Mr. Murphy, "I hear there's an exhibition game—the Sox versus a bunch of blindfolded kindergarteners in body casts. The Sox may actually have a chance."

"Can someone please tell me why," Mr. Murphy begins, "I

have to put up with this in my own house? It's an injustice, you know that?" He reaches under the couch and pulls out a white bag. "Good thing I'm such a good sport! Come here, girls! I got you each a little something." He pulls out two baseball hats. First, he hands Toni a pink Yankees hat.

"Pink? You got me pink?"

"Yeah. I thought it would be nice on a pretty girl like you."

Wow. I didn't think anything could stop Toni from talking, but that does. Miracle.

Then he hands me a green Boston hat with a cream-colored shamrock on the brim. "I thought I'd get you the Irish one, ye young lass, Carley Connors!" he says. It makes me smile. I really like how it's Irish. The bright green reminds me of the trees. And besides that, I feel like I'm a part of something special.

As I put on the hat, I think about my conversation with Mr. Murphy. I think how he really does need to come home. How his family needs him.

I also think that maybe I'm not supposed to be able to save my mother. Maybe I'm supposed to save myself first.

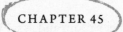

CHAPTER 45

On the Line

Mrs. MacAvoy waits outside for me. I go to her car and get into the backseat.

"Hello, Carley."

"Hey."

We pull away from the curb. "So, you know why I've come to take you to see your mom today?"

"Because I'm her one and only? The love of her life? The light in her days?"

She sounds kind of sad. "Well, I guess you're still angry."

And I think how I'm not, really. Not like I used to be. The Murphys calm me, I guess. "Sorry."

"Why did you run from your mother's room?" she asks.

"Training for a marathon." I don't know what it is about this woman that keeps me from giving her a straight answer.

She sighs, long and deep. "Well, she wants to see you. There is something that she really needs to tell you."

Well, I guess it's my lucky day.

I march into my mother's room and ask, "What's going on?"

"So, that's the way it's going to be, then?" my mother says, never taking her eyes from the TV.

"Hey, last I heard, you were done with me."

"Carley, you're not the smartypants you think you are. If it weren't for me—"

"Yeah, I know," I interrupt. "All those things you did for me? Cooking dinner for me. Giving up all those parties and dates." I point at her and slap my knee. "Oh, wait. You didn't give up any of that stuff. Not once."

"You're hopeless. Just hopeless."

My mother calls me hopeless a lot when I'm not what she wants me to be—more like her. I have always curled up inside when I've heard it, but now I know that she's wrong.

"Carley, it's not that I don't love you," she continues. "You do know I love you, right? I know I made mistakes. But I . . . I love my girl so much." She starts to cry. "Please. Please remember that always."

There's something about her voice I've never heard before, and it worries me. Almost like she is pleading with me. Pleading with me to never forget that she loves me. It sounds like good-bye.

"Maybe you belong with these Murphys," she says.

And I thought I did until I hear her say it. I do love them. So much. But . . . "Mom. What are you talking about? You're just going to put me out with the trash?"

Her voice is never quiet but it is now. "There's a difference between putting out the trash and letting a bird out of its cage."

"What cage?" I panic because I know when my mother means business. "Mom. Remember how you'd hold Oreos over your eyes and they'd leave brown circles and you'd look like a raccoon? Remember how funny that was?"

Her whole face softens. Her body relaxes. Then I see everything stiffen in her and her eyes almost close. "Did you ever think that raising a kid is hard? That maybe I just can't anymore?"

"You can't mean that!"

She stares into my eyes like she'll never look away. "Listen, Carley. I wanted you to come because . . ."

"What?"

"Never mind that. You'll have . . . They'll be . . ." Then she looks away quick. Her tone becomes cutting. "Listen here, Carley. I have a life of my own in Vegas. One that doesn't involve a kid following me around. I'm all ready to sign the papers."

I run again. Down the stairs and through the lobby, right by Mrs. MacAvoy, and out the doors of the facility. Me running and her trying to keep up. Out of breath, she asks, "Carley, what happened?"

We get into the car. "Nothing. I want to get back to the house."

She stares at me for a while. Trying to figure if she can get it out of me, I guess. Finally, she turns and starts the car.

When we arrive at the Murphys' house, I jump out of the car

and burst through the front door and into the kitchen. Mrs. Murphy spins around and panic falls onto her face. "Are you okay?"

"No. No, I'm not okay!" I scream because I know she'll let me. "My mother. She's signing me away to foster care. Forever."

"What?" Mrs. MacAvoy asks, coming into the kitchen.

"That doesn't make sense," Mrs. Murphy says.

"You've met me. Of course it makes sense. You can't wait to get rid of me too."

She tears up. "You *know* that isn't true."

"Carley, I don't know what just happened with your mother," Mrs. MacAvoy says, "but I do know she wants you back. You know she was beaten so badly that they weren't sure she'd even live, never mind walk. I mean, it's a miracle that she's doing as well as she is."

"Let's put her face on Mount Rushmore, then."

"Listen, Carley. She risked her life for you. From what I understand, the charges against her were dropped because they got Dennis to admit that she hadn't helped him. When your mom realized that he was going to seriously hurt you, she tried to stop him, and so he beat her too."

And then I remembered. Finally, I remembered.

"Mom! No!" I screamed as I looked back over my shoulder. Dennis charged me and my mother's grasp on my ankle tightened. Dennis kicked me and the room spun.

My mother stood, but stumbled. She shrieked, "No! No! You monster! You leave her alone!" I heard scuffling around the room. My mother hit Dennis with a vase. He yelled and swore and my mother cried. Then he really hurt her.

Not long after, I remember someone else screaming, "Get down! Get down on the floor! Now!" It must have been the police talking to Dennis. I heard them wrestle him to the floor. I heard him swearing, saying this was a family matter and to mind their own business. I heard the clicking of the handcuffs.

Someone knelt in front of me, but I was too tired to open my eyes all the way. Someone with shiny black shoes and a sad voice.

That was when I wondered if people like me go to heaven.

I turn to Mrs. MacAvoy and Mrs. Murphy, but I'm afraid to open my mouth.

"You know, Carley," Mrs. Murphy says, "your mom knew what she was doing. She put her life on the line for yours. That's what a real mother does."

"A mother who really *loves* you, Carley," Mrs. MacAvoy adds.

CHAPTER 46

The Giving . . . Uh, I Mean . . . The Living Tree

Later that night I sit on the front steps. It's warm out and the trees blow back and forth. I think about how they bend in the wind but rarely break.

I think about heroes. How they do the hard things that no one else can do.

I think about Mr. Murphy and his deep sandpapery laugh and how he risks his life so strangers can live. What kind of person goes to work every day not knowing if he'll come home?

And most of all, I think about Mrs. Murphy—the way she gives everything, does everything, holds us all up. Meeting her makes me feel like God has started paying attention. The way she reached in, pulled me out, dusted me off, and said that I only need to be the great person that I am.

I hear the door open behind me. It's Mrs. Murphy.

"Mind if I join you?" Mrs. Murphy asks.

"Sure." I move over.

She sits next to me. "So what're you doing?"

"Thinking."

"Do you mind if I ask about what?"

"My new book. It's called *Giving Tree Meets Chainsaw and Becomes Coffee Table*."

"Oh boy." She takes a deep breath. "So we're in that kind of mood, huh?"

"I thought you'd think it was funny." I wait before I finish, trying to decide if I should. "I still hate that book, though."

"I understand."

Mrs. Murphy's soft expression makes me think how the tree in that book shouldn't be a stump; it should be bigger and greener from loving the little boy.

"So, are you nervous about seeing your mother again tomorrow, now that you know what really happened?"

"Well . . . yeah. I guess, a little." I think about my mother and all that happened that night and how I misjudged her. How she risked herself to save me in the end. How she must have been afraid and did it anyway.

There's a long silence. Finally I ask, "I'm never going to see you again, am I? I mean, assuming I go back to my mother like Mrs. MacAvoy predicts. I won't see you again."

"Well . . . Mrs. MacAvoy thinks that you need some time to realign yourself with your own mom. Without . . . the distraction of us. It's for your own good, she says."

"But no one would have to know! I could call you secretly. Or you could call me?" I know her answer even as I suggest this. The woman who loves rules would never break one as big as this.

"It's for your own protection."

"That's garbage."

"It will take time, Carley. Be patient with yourself."

That sounds hard.

"I've been thinking, though," she continues.

"Yeah?" I don't look at her.

"I hope you go to college."

"College? You're kidding me. People like *me* don't go to college."

"You mean bright, creative people?"

"My mom would never let me do that."

"If you wanted to go, your mother wouldn't be able to stop you. True, it would be harder, but there are scholarships and grants. Talk to the counselors at your school. They can help you navigate all of that. But *you* have to take charge. You, Carley."

Can I imagine myself doing that? I'm afraid to think of the future. And then I think of Daniel. How I stood in the driveway giving him a speech on courage. About being afraid and doing it anyway, because you can't score points if you don't take shots.

"And you know, Carley . . ." Her tone wraps its arm around me. "I know that you'll find it difficult to leave us . . . but try to think of it not as leaving us but as going to something new. Maybe you've learned some things here. You know, about what you want."

I look at her.

"You can have this for real, you know—not just wishing you could have what others have."

How does she know I think about that?

"You can go to college. Have a career you love. You can find yourself married to a goofball Red Sox fanatic." She laughs. "You may even find yourself chasing three wild boys. You can make this life if you want it. Any life that you want."

"But . . . I want *this* family." I wish I could lean on her.

"I know," she whispers.

It seems like too much. How could I do all these things she says like it's nothing? I gather the strength to really look at her. "I don't want to go. Please don't make me."

"Not up to me, sweetheart." She swallows her tears, I think. "And it will be awful when you go. But I'm so happy you've been a part of our lives, Carley. It's better that we all met each other than not, don't you think?"

I nod.

"Yeah," Mrs. Murphy whispers, looking up at the dark sky.

I can't stop thinking about the college thing. "I guess I'd like to be a teacher," I turn to her. "Help kids like you did."

"It's just a matter of making a decision and following through. You're smart enough and special enough to pull it off." She bumps my shoulder with hers, and I think of Toni.

She takes a deep breath like she's getting ready to lift something heavy. "Remember that friend I had in foster care who had a rough time? That . . . was *me*."

"But you seem so normal!"

She laughs again. "Well, I like to think so." She looks me in the eye. "Carley, it wasn't my fault I was in foster care. When I was young I had this crazy idea that it was, but when I got older, I realized I didn't have that kind of power. My parents did."

"Were you in a house like this?"

"I bounced around foster care for four years. Not optimal situations. But it forced me to decide what kind of life I wanted. And I went after it when I was old enough."

I feel betrayed. "You should have told me."

"I wanted your stay here to be about *you*—not me."

Wow.

We sit for a long time until she asks, "What's that mischievous smile about?"

"Well, I was thinking that . . . maybe if I go to college and *do* become a teacher someday . . ."

She waits for me.

". . . Maybe I'll be someone's hero. You know, like Michael Eric's sign. I know. That sounds dumb, huh?"

She puts her pointer finger under my chin and lifts my face to look her in the eye. "That's not dumb. Not at all. I have no doubt that you'll do whatever you put your mind to."

All of a sudden, I just have to stand. And something I've never known before grows inside and rises up through the center of me.

I stand tall, looking back at Mrs. Murphy. "I'll have a happy life someday," I say. And they're more than just words. My insides are steel. Unbreakable. "It won't always be like this for me. Someday, I will have a happy life. I swear I will."

Her eyes tear up. "That's right, Carley. And don't you *ever* settle for anything less."

CHAPTER 47

One for the Murphys

I stand in the doorway to my mom's room, holding a package of Oreos, and I watch how she's all curled up with her back to me. How we must look alike that way.

"Mom?" I ask.

She jolts a little but doesn't answer me. I step into the room.

"Mom? Why didn't you tell me? Why didn't you tell me what really happened that night? Is it true? Did you save me?"

I hear her crying. Harder now.

"Mom, it's okay. Why didn't you tell me?"

She rolls onto her back and sits up. "Oh, Carley, I don't know. I guess I thought you'd remember. And . . . to tell the truth . . ." She clears her throat. "Then when I first saw you again, I hardly knew you. I mean, you were dressed so nice and your hair and . . ."

She stares at her lap and cries some more. "That MacAvoy woman told me that the family who had you really took to you.

That you were doing real good and making good marks in school and had a best friend." She looks at me. "And I just thought that . . ."

I wait as she goes silent. Finally, I ask, "What, Mom? What is it?"

"I thought it wouldn't make a difference what I'd done helping you that night. Not after what I'd done before. Oh, Carley. I can't believe I did that."

I stuff my hands in my pockets.

"And I thought that if those people wanted to keep you, that . . ." She puts her hands over her face. "That you would have a better life without me."

"But *you're* my mom!"

She lets out a bunch of air all at once. "Then you don't want that Murphy woman to be your mom instead?"

The wind's been knocked out of me, but I try to smile. "She would never call me at school on my birthday."

She laughs through her tears. "Oh, my Carley, I'm so sorry I missed your birthday!"

For the first time, I am too. "So, you couldn't walk, huh?" I say, staring at her legs under a white sheet.

"No, but I can walk now. I'm just about done with the walker too. They say they never seen someone work as hard as me. I should be out in a week or so."

A week? I only have a week? "So we're going to move back to Grandpa's?"

"Well, I've been thinking on this hard, and I think we're Vegas girls, you and I. We have to be in a place where there's life, things going on, you know? My cousin will give me cash for the condo. It will work out finer than fine, Carley. You wait and see."

Leaving Connecticut? My head tells me my mom is my home, but the rest of me says I belong here with the Murphys and my best friend.

"So start collecting your things," she says. "We'll be heading back soon. You'll see. It will be great. It will be just like it was."

I back up against the wall.

As I walk into the kitchen, Mrs. Murphy looks up from the counter to see how I am, and it hits me again how much I will miss her. She says, "Hey. Are you doing okay? How did it go? Is your mom doing better?"

I like how she asks how I am before everything else. "We worked things out."

"Good. That's good news, Carley."

"Yeah."

"You know, Carley, if I could talk to your mom, I'd thank her for raising such a great person. She's made mistakes, I know. But she's obviously done something right too."

I blurt out, "My mom is probably going to being released next week. Then she wants us to move back to Las Vegas." I focus on her face to see if she cares.

"That's terrific news for you and your mom, Carley. I'm happy for you both."

I am sad that she reacts this way until I look at her face and see she's forcing it.

"Not so happy for us, though," Mrs. Murphy adds. She

watches the floor as she leans against the counter and I realize she never looks down like that. Her voice is a whisper now. "We *will* miss you . . . terribly."

I think of my mom and then of Mrs. Murphy. How she's both strong and gentle; the two, twisted together like soft-serve ice cream. I wish hard that there could be two of me. One for my mother.

And one for the Murphys.

CHAPTER 48

Soft Place to Land

Over my last few days with the Murphys I keep staring at them, thinking about how I'll miss them, wondering if they'll remember me. Wondering if I'll ever see them again.

While I was helping Mrs. Murphy with dinner, I asked her if I could come see her when I'm all grown up. Like if I showed up one day without telling her, if I just came searching for her, if it would be okay.

She cleared her throat. "There would never be a day when I wouldn't want to see you."

Tonight, the house is quiet except for the audience laughter that comes from Jay Leno playing in Mrs. Murphy's bedroom. I've always thought it was funny that on the nights Mr. Murphy is at the station, Jay Leno takes his place.

I think about Mom. I am freaked about the whole thing. Going back to Vegas. Even if things are okay, it won't be like here.

No apple pies or fresh beds. The days of someone taking care of me are over.

I remember how my mom used to say we were the same. That the apple doesn't fall far from the tree. I think, now, that although the apple can come from the tree, it can land on the ground and roll down a hill and end up in a totally different place.

A . . . totally . . . different place.

I steel myself and look up at my hero sign. I'm going to put my head down and do what I have to. I so wish, though, that I could do it with the Murphys, but I know that I belong with my mom. As Mrs. Murphy says, family comes first.

Doesn't it?

Heading back to Vegas could be okay. I mean, I had some friends there. I think of the looks on their faces when I turn up again. But there's a problem. One big thing that worries me.

I am different now.

I . . . am a Murphy.

I know not in name, but I can't imagine life without them. Without Michael Eric and his crooked smile. Adam with his flaming red hair and pockets of cars. Daniel—intense Daniel who is more like me than I would ever have imagined. And Mr. Murphy, that crazy Sox fan who managed to soften up Toni Byars.

But it's Julie Murphy who will keep a chunk of me here. I have a terrible longing in my stomach; there's one thing I need from her before I go, but I don't know how to ask. I lean my forehead against the glass of the window and push—not hard enough to break it but hard enough to feel like I could.

I think back to the very beginning here, when I watched Mrs. Murphy hold and rock Michael Eric over such a small thing as a hurt hand and couldn't understand it. Now, I long for a piece of it. I know this will be the last time I'll get a chance to know what that feels like.

My feet do the walking as I try to decide. A mechanical kind of walk. Twenty steps to Mrs. Murphy's bedroom is a good even number and a multiple of ten.

She's watching Leno and laughing. She waves me in.

She wears one of her happy shirts. There are ten stripes across the front, and I count them over and over. Over and over.

She studies me for a bit before saying, "Tell me." Her voice coaxes a child from her hiding place. "Tell me what's going on."

I shake my head.

She walks to the other side of the room while I stare at Mr. Murphy's picture—his Navy picture—and remember the day I smashed the glass.

She turns the television off and then stands in front of me. I hold my breath.

She reaches out and lays her hand on my arm. I jump but force my feet to stay put. I close my eyes. One, two, three . . .

"Let me give you a hug, Carley. I think you could use one."

I want one so bad, but I shake my head.

"It'll be okay," she says.

I am stiff and glued in place. "I want you to be proud of me. I don't want to be weak. I want you to remember me being strong."

She laughs a little. "There isn't a shred of weakness in you. Besides, now don't you think there's a lot of strength in letting people help you?" She leans toward me just the slightest bit. "It's easier to lock yourself away, Carley. It takes strength to face things that scare you."

"It's just that I don't want you to see me like that. You know. A mess. Crying like a baby."

"You mean human?"

"I don't want to disappoint you."

"What? You *can't* disappoint me, Carley." She leans to look me in the eye.

I look up at where the ceiling meets the wall. I stuff two fists into my pockets. "I can't. I don't know how. I mean, I don't do that."

"Sure you do."

"No . . . I really don't."

She puts her arms out. "Come here. If you're not going to cry with me, who're you going to cry with?"

I don't have an answer.

"C'mon, now. It'll be okay, Carley. I promise."

While my head struggles for what to do, my feet move forward and Mrs. Murphy's shoulder becomes a soft place to land.

Her arms come around me and rest on my back. I panic and stiffen and pull away hard, but she won't let me go. "It'll be okay, honey," she whispers. "Stay with me."

There's a fire beneath my skin that makes me very afraid. I turn my head, searching the wall for something to count, but there's just the softness of her shirt and the sound of her voice. The warmth of her breath on my ear.

She holds me tight, rocking back and forth a bit.

My body feels like it isn't mine. Strange. My eyes water. My shoulders shake. My own sounds make me want to run but I *can't* let go. I squeeze her harder and harder. The way you hold the safety bar on a roller coaster when it dips. I close my eyes and bury my face in her shoulder and hold on tight.

"That's right, honey," she whispers again. "It'll be better now."

Where once I would've run, I'm now still. I stand, collapsing in her arms, depending on this woman to hold me up.

And she does.

I wake up slowly, embarrassed about the night before. How Mrs. Murphy walked me into my room after I couldn't cry any more or hardly even stand. How she folded the blankets back and tucked me in. How I mumbled that I felt like a five-year-old and how she told me that it was about time I got to be a five-year-old.

How when she turned to go, I reached out without thinking and grabbed her arm. And when I couldn't say anything, she simply said, "I'll stay."

I fell asleep knowing she was sitting on the bed watching me and knowing she wouldn't leave till I fell asleep. I tried to stay awake, but I can't remember anything so tiring as crying.

When I get downstairs, I'm still in my clothes from the day before. Mrs. Murphy is at the sink. When she turns to me, I feel a little silly. Until her face softens and she looks at me like she's seeing the best thing ever. "Hey," she says. "How're you doing today, huh?"

"Fine."

She laughs. "Oh, that's right. You're always fine."

"I'm sorry," I blurt out.

She looks so surprised. "Sorry? About what?"

"About last night." I know what she'll say, but I want to hear it.

"You don't have to apologize to me for anything. Not ever."

"I don't know why I did that. I really don't do stuff like that." It's hard not to look away. "Well, not usually anyway."

She smiles without showing any teeth and takes a breath. "Well, I think sometimes the heart just leads the way."

I remember a time when that would have made me laugh in disgust, but it did feel like that. And I guess I don't regret it or anything, but I'm still embarrassed. "Okay," I answer.

Her gaze lingers for a couple of seconds before she smiles with a little suspicion in her eyes and says, "Good, then." When she winks at me, I think about how her kids have always known this warmth inside. And how I know it too now.

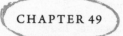

CHAPTER 49

Someone's Hero

Mrs. Murphy is baking an apple pie.

I know it's for me and it's for a party. Not a good party—a going-away party. I never thought I'd have a reason to dread one of her apple pies, but I do now.

The kitchen has been decorated by the boys. There's crepe paper tied and taped to everything. Michael Eric made a giant sad face with huge blue tears. It's so easy for him to express that stuff. Before meeting the Murphys, it wouldn't have occurred to me to draw something like that for anyone.

I take my spot on the counter. Mrs. Murphy takes a green bean casserole out of the oven, then turns to me and asks, "Do you need anything?"

I shake my head. Then I say it. "You know, for the record, I don't really want to go. I mean, I'm happy that my mom is okay and all but . . ."

Her eyes are shiny now. "I know," she says, patting my knee. "I know." She bites the inside of her cheek as she turns and takes my favorite dish, which I now call "Mrs. Murphy's Famous Chicken Thingie," out of the oven.

"I was hoping for lasagna," I say.

Sadness turns to surprise for a second before she says, "Oh, be quiet!" and hits me on the leg with the oven mitt.

"Nice. Beat up on the foster kid," I say, laughing. But then I remember that she, too, is a foster kid. So many things make sense now.

Mrs. Murphy smiles like part of her is missing. She leans in and drops her voice. "You just *remember*, Carley Connors, you were a *part* of this family. And you'll *always* be in my life, even if I'm not in yours."

I hear the words, but I also hear it in her voice. My stomach twists and I brush away a tear as soon as it leaves my eye. I can't remember anyone ever saying such a thing to me. I can't remember anyone else ever looking at me like that. So deep and nice and right into the middle of me.

She puts her hand on my knee. "You remember that. *Promise* me."

I nod, holding my breath because I'm afraid that if I breathe, I'll lose it.

"It's okay," she says.

My stomach muscles harden. "I don't want the boys to see me blubbering."

She laughs out loud. "You mean that little drop of water? I

don't think that constitutes blubbering. Besides, they're used to me. They wouldn't even notice *that!*"

The doorbell rings. I answer it and find Toni wearing her pink Yankees hat. "Surprise!" she yells, smacks me on the arm, and heads for the kitchen.

"Hey, Mrs. Murphy," she says.

"And hey to you! I like that hat!"

I'm so glad she's here.

Mr. Murphy pipes up from the family room. "Love the hat!"

"Yeah," Toni says. "I decided that the Yankees can overcome anything. Even pink."

"You look nice in pink," I say. "It sets off your eyes."

"Don't torment me, Connors. Besides, pink would only set off my eyes if I were a vampire or something."

I laugh at her. "I think you'd be more like one of those sweet, white bunnies."

"Watch yourself, Connors." She smiles, but it's sad underneath.

Everyone comes to the table, and it gets loud. Mrs. Murphy is running around, pouring drinks.

"Do you want me to help?" I ask.

"No! This is your night. You just relax." She sits down at the table. "Jack, why don't we turn off the Sox game tonight? This is a special occasion."

He stands.

"It's okay," I say. "It would seem weird without it on."

"You're something special, Carley," he says, winking at me,

"but Julie is right." He turns the TV off and comes back. He pulls in his chair. "Who wants to do grace tonight?"

Michael Eric yells, "Me! I'll do it!"

"Okay then, Michael Eric. Take it away."

We all hold hands, and I think of the first night I did this here. How I prayed to leave then, and now I'd pray to stay.

"Dear God," Michael Eric begins. "Thank you for our food and toys and baseball and stuff. Please let the Red Sox win so Daddy isn't crabby, and please let us keep Carley here. If you can't or you're busy and stuff, then I'll ask Santa. Amen."

Toni looks sad, and Adam asks, "Mom? Would Santa leave Carley under our tree?"

"I don't think Santa can give a person for Christmas, honey," Mrs. Murphy says. She still holds my hand from the prayer.

"Santa can do anything!" Michael Eric exclaims, his mouth already full of food.

"You're a piece of work there, Michael Eric," his dad says. "God broke the mold when he made you."

Daniel answers, "Yeah. Broke it over his head."

"Shut up!" Michael Eric yells.

"Now, now," their mom says. She gives my hand a firm squeeze before she finally lets go.

After we finish dinner, Mrs. Murphy produces two apple pies. She hands me a serving fork and puts a whole pie in front of me. "I know. I don't expect you to eat the whole thing," she says. "But I wanted you to know it's all yours. Your very own."

"Well, not all yours. Right, Connors?" Toni asks. "Being the friend that I am, I'll help."

So Toni and I work on the one pie while the Murphys work on the other one.

"Hey, Carley," Daniel says. "Remember when Mom made cupcakes and one was missing? Remember how Michael Eric told everyone he didn't take it, but he had chocolate frosting all over his neck?" Everyone laughs.

"What about that wicked pickup game Daniel and I had with those guys who used to give him a hard time?" I say.

Daniel smiles. "Oh wait—the best was you teaching Jimmy Partin a lesson." Michael Eric and Adam go nuts.

Uh-oh.

"Wait. What's this about Jimmy Partin?" Mr. Murphy asks.

As I try to say that it was nothing, Michael Eric says, "He was being a jerk face and so Carley hung him in a tree!"

Mrs. Murphy is wide-eyed. "You *hung* him . . . in a *tree*?"

I blurt out, "By his overalls straps; he was fine. Would it help if I said he deserved it?"

Toni says, "It would help me. Sure."

"Me too," adds Mr. Murphy.

Mrs. Murphy shakes her head. "I think I'm glad that I didn't know." She smirks. "So that's why he leaves Michael Eric alone these days?"

I nod.

Michael Eric and Adam spend some time doing Jimmy Partin imitations. Soon most of the pie is gone, and I walk Toni to the door.

"Well, this is it," I say.

"Deep, Connors. Very deep."

"I don't know what to say. I feel horrible."

"Yeah. Me too." Toni stuffs her hands into her jeans pockets.

"Hey, tell Rainer that I'll miss him!" I laugh.

"Rainer is back to himself. He told me that you'll never be anything but a roll stuffer. He's such a simp!"

I laugh, wondering if she knows how much I'll miss her. I put my life on the line, step up, and give her a hug.

She gives a stiff hug back but pulls away quick. "One more thing, Connors. Because I want you to remember me." She steps outside, jumps into the bushes, and comes up with a wrapped box. She holds it out.

"A present? Really?" I don't hesitate to open it. Inside is her crazy embroidered New York jacket. "I can't take this, Toni, it's your favorite jacket."

"That's precisely why you need to take it."

I know I should force her to keep it, but I'm really happy to have it. Not only the jacket but the memory of her holding it out to me, looking miserable and like it's Christmas all at the same time.

"Here's the other one," she says, handing me a new *Wicked* CD. I smile.

"Track eighteen, Connors. It's all about track eighteen."

I bend over and unlace my high tops.

"What are you doing?" she asks.

I look up. "You have to take these."

"Some trade, Connors. Sneakers so disgusting they can probably walk by themselves." She laughs.

"So I was thinking, Toni," I tell her. "Someday you could be

Elphaba. On stage. In New York. And when that happens, I'll be there to see you."

"Really?" she asks. "Ya think so? Me? Elphaba in New York?"

"Yeah. And I promise I'll come," I tell her. "Because we'll be friends 'til we're old and deaf and blind and crippled."

"Wow, Connors," she says, sniffing. "You sound like you're going to be a real blast."

We both laugh. And then she hugs me fast and hard, turns and runs. Out and across the grass with my high tops under her arm. I dread how much I'm going to miss her.

Putting on her New York jacket, I walk back into the kitchen. I must look miserable, because Mrs. Murphy comes over and rubs my back. Then she says, "I've got something for you too." She hands me the gift, but as soon as I see it, I know what it is. When I reached for it this morning to add my eightieth tally, it was gone.

I peel the paper off and draw my fingers over the letters that spell BE SOMEONE'S HERO. Then I flip it over and glance at the tally marks written on the back.

"Yeah, I noticed that," she says. "I can't imagine why that's there."

I half smile, thinking about how it started as a tally of days in captivity and how, now, it feels like a tally of days at home.

I look up at Mrs. Murphy and say, "Thank you," wishing that I could say something more—something so perfect that she'd remember it forever. I step up to her, a little afraid. I rest my head on her shoulder and give her a hug. I say, "Thanks for the present. I'll take it as a *sign*."

She laughs. "What a clip you are with that sense of humor of yours!" Then she squeezes a little harder. "You know, sometimes I think it's me who should thank you."

"You mean once I stopped picking fights with waiters and stuffing rolls behind cushions?"

She laughs again. "Oh boy. Let's not resurrect *that* memory!"

I step back and look at my sign again. Feel the smoothness of the wood. "I've been thinking about what we were talking about. You know, college?" I look her in the eye. "I'll get there. I'll try hard to be someone's hero."

"Oh, Carley," she says. "You already are."

CHAPTER 50

A Great and Terrible Thing

I've packed the suitcase that Mrs. Murphy said I could keep because "you never know when you'll need a good suitcase." I'm hoping that I don't need one for a while.

There's a soft knock on the door, and sadness washes over me, along with the understanding that this is it. I'm really leaving them.

"Come in."

The door opens, but I don't turn around.

"Carley?" It's Daniel.

He comes in, holding his Celtics basketball. He steps up to me and holds it out.

"I'm sorry, Daniel. I don't think we have time to play now."

"I want you to take it."

"Why?"

"Because those losers in Las Vegas probably don't sell Celtics basketballs. Who do you root for out there? The Utah Jazz? I'd rather go to jail."

We shuffle our feet, looking to fill the silence.

"It was really nice that you helped me, Carley. I know I wouldn't be playing this good if you hadn't . . . helped me . . . and . . ."

"It's okay, Daniel. Really."

"I'm sorry I was a jerk to you."

"Well . . . I actually understand. And I was a jerk, too. Don't sweat it."

He nods.

"Hey, if your mom ever lets you online, look me up, okay?"

He has a funny expression. "I heard my mom tell my dad that we're not supposed to contact you."

I let out all of my air.

He smiles. "But I will anyway."

"Good." I swallow hard.

He hands me the ball. "Here. I signed it for you."

I spin the ball over, and I see written in black, crooked cursive, "Carley—Thanks for everything! Dan 'The Man' Murphy."

I don't know what to say, but I do worry that if Daniel can get me feeling blubbery, the rest of them are really going to kill me.

I can sense his mom is in the doorway without even looking. "Carley. It's time to go, honey."

Honey.

I pick up my bag and walk toward the door, but I can't look at her. My arm brushes her as I go by. "I may decorate my room like this at home. I think I like it."

"Is that so?" She sounds far away.

I reach the stairs. Thirteen steps to the bottom.

At the bottom of the stairs, Michael Eric is holding Mr. Longneck under his arm. He and Adam become attached to my legs. I get down on my knees.

"Here," Adam says, holding out a Matchbox car. "Daniel was going to give you a present, and I wanted to too."

I take the Matchbox car from him. "Thanks, Adam. Are you sure you want to give it away?"

"It's broken anyways."

I crack up. "Thanks." I hold out my hand and he slaps me five.

I give Michael Eric a hug. "Hey, bud. Thanks for teaching me to play superheroes. I had a really great time with you."

"I don't have a present for you," he says sadly.

"What are you talking about? I'll always remember the great times we had playing superheroes. You just keep those bad guys in line, okay?"

He nods, and I wrap him up; I have a hard time letting him go.

Mrs. Murphy looks at Jack, points at the boys, and moves her head to the side. He understands her hint as he says, "Okay, guys. Let's leave your mom alone for a few minutes." He gives me a stiff hug, but then messes up my hair—the way he hugs his boys—and I know this is a compliment. "Take care of yourself, Carley."

"Thanks," I say. He disappears with the boys, but I can still hear Michael Eric's protests.

"Mrs. MacAvoy is waiting in her car outside," Mrs. Murphy says.

I nod.

"I'm going to miss you," she says.

Looking at her and knowing this is it, I feel like a piece of me dies. "Me too . . . I mean, I'll miss you too. Thanks for everything."

"You're very welcome."

"I mean everything."

She nods. Biting the inside of her cheek, she opens the front door.

"And thanks again for the sign," I say. "I love it."

She nods again. Trying not to cry, I think.

I'm not sure if I want her to lose it or not as I say, "You've been mine, ya know. Hero, I mean."

She pulls me in and kisses me on the cheek, then holds my face in her hands. I force myself to look into her eyes because I want to remember. I just have to remember.

"Oh, Carley. I *know* that you'll be fine. You'll make a good life for yourself, I just *know* you will."

I'm surprised that I believe her.

I tell myself to turn around, and I order my feet to move. When I look up again, I am at the bottom of the stairs standing on the sidewalk. I want to run back up to her so much that I don't dare look at her. I focus on Mrs. MacAvoy waiting in her car at the end of the driveway.

I think back to when Mrs. Murphy told me that you regret the things you don't do more than the things you do. This gives me permission, and I am up the three steps in one leap. I wrap my arms around her without looking at her face and rest my head on her shoulder. "I . . . *love* you, Mrs. Murphy."

I can feel her shake as she cries. "I love you too, Carley."

Hearing her say it. Knowing she means it. Makes it so hard to go. "I'll never forget you . . . I mean, never ever."

I peel away only because I have to, but she doesn't let go easily. I swing around quickly and jump down the steps, reaching the driveway and heading toward the car.

A yell comes from far behind me. "Carley! You have to stay! You just *have* to!"

Michael Eric comes around the side of the house and down the driveway to me. His Thomas the Tank Engine cape is twisting behind him.

He waves a piece of paper. "I made you a present!" He hands me the paper and I flip it over. It has "C-R-L-Y" in red crayon across the top and a drawing of what I think is me as Super High Tops Girl.

"Hey! You did a great job writing my name!" I wrap my arms around him a last time. "It's awesome, Michael Eric. I'll keep it forever!"

"Come here, buddy," his dad calls. Michael Eric gives my leg a kiss and then hops and runs up the hill to the garage, where his father scoops him up.

Adam and Daniel come around the corner and join their dad. Daniel half waves. I wave back and turn away as my eyes water.

And then I stop. I know I need to go as I stand facing Mrs. MacAvoy's car; I want to be able to leave on my own, though— before she calls me. But still, I turn back to look at Mrs. Murphy.

One more time.

And I just can't breathe.

I don't wave or move or say anything. Right now, I just want to take a picture with me. I know that even a long time from now, I'll remember her standing in front of a bright white door with a happy shirt and teary, red, blotchy cheeks. I'll remember how the breeze moved her hair back and forth across her forehead. I'll remember how she shook her head the tiniest bit.

But most of all, I'll remember how she loved me.

I turn away, knowing that I might never get to see Julie Murphy ever again.

But I will *know* her for the rest of my life.

ACKNOWLEDGMENTS

My affection and gratitude for the talented Erin Murphy, who, besides having the most perfect name ever, believed in this book and its author. You're the best, Murphy. You really are.

My boundless thanks to Nancy Paulsen, my supportive, talented, and collaborative editor, who exceeded all of my dreams of having a publisher. Thank you for taking Carley under your wing and treating her so well.

Huge thanks, also, to the talented team at Nancy Paulsen Books/Penguin: Cecilia Yung, Ryan Thomann, Danielle Delaney, and Sara Kreger.

For Rere, who gave me more than I could ever list here.

In loving memory of my brother, Michael Eric Mullaly.

For anyone who lovingly cares for other people's children, including Sr. Ginger Smith, O.P., The Smith Families, and Pete and Dot Steeves and their children: Peter, Fred, Jen, Joe, Amy, and Patrick.

With tons of love and appreciation for the following people, whose support was no small piece of this debut novel: Rick Mullaly, Jill Mullaly, Michael T. Mullaly, Megan Mullaly, Karen Mullaly Blass, Suzannah Blass, Carol Boehm Hunt, Susan Rheaume, Kathy Martin Benzi, Danielle Neary, Franca and Emily Silliman, Kelly Henderschedt and Emma/Lucy/Rosie, Francis X. Miller, Samantha Eileen Miller, Patricia Reilly Giff, Lucia Zimmitti, Jeanne Zulick Ferruolo, Bette Anne Rieth, Laurie Smith Murphy, Liz Goulet Dubois, Barbara Johansen-Newman, Mary Pierce, and my students and fellow faculty members at Gilead Hill School in Hebron, Connecticut.

Huge hugs to the Gango, who have enriched my life so much. On this wonderful journey, you have been one of the greatest gifts.

Another nod to Greg, my best friend and only love.

And finally, but of monumental importance, for Kimmy and Kyle—two of my most favorite people on the planet. Thanks for making my life even more magnificent than I could have ever imagined. Love you both infinity times around Pluto.

TURN THE PAGE FOR A LOOK AT

LYNDA MULLALY HUNT'S

NEXT NOVEL

Text copyright © Lynda Mullaly Hunt

CHAPTER 1

In Trouble Again

It's always there. Like the ground underneath my feet.

"Well, Ally? Are you going to write or aren't you?" Mrs. Hall asks.

If my teacher were mean it would be easier.

"C'mon," she says. "I know you can do it."

"What if I told you that I was going to climb a tree using only my teeth? Would you say I could *do it* then?"

Oliver laughs, throwing himself on his desk like it's a fumbled football.

Shay groans. "Ally, why can't you just act normal for once?"

Near her, Albert, a bulky kid who's worn the same thing every day—a dark T-shirt that reads *Flint*—sits up straight. Like he's waiting for a firecracker to go off.

Mrs. Hall sighs. "C'mon, now. I'm only asking for one page describing yourself."

I can't think of anything worse than having to describe myself. I'd rather write about something more positive. Like throwing up at your own birthday party.

"It's important," she says. "It's so your new teacher can get to know you."

I know that, and it's exactly why I don't want to do it. Teachers are like the machines that take quarters for bouncy balls. You know what you're going to get. Yet, you don't know, too.

"And," she says. "All that doodling of yours, Ally. If you weren't drawing all the time, your work might be done. Please put it away."

Embarrassed, I slide my drawings underneath my blank writing assignment. I've been drawing pictures of myself being shot out of a cannon. It would be easier than school. Less painful.

"C'mon," she says, moving my lined paper toward me. "Just do your best."

Seven schools in seven years and they're all the same. Whenever I do my best, they tell me I don't try hard enough. Too messy. Careless spelling. Annoyed that the same word is spelled different ways on the same page. And the headaches. I always get headaches from looking

2

at the brightness of dark letters on white pages for too long.

Mrs. Hall clears her throat.

The rest of the class is getting tired of me again. Chairs slide. Loud sighs. Maybe they think I can't hear their words: *Freak. Dumb. Loser.*

I wish she'd just go hang by Albert, the walking Google page who'd get a better grade than me if he just blew his nose into the paper.

The back of my neck heats up.

I don't get it. She always let me slide. It must be because these are for the new teacher and she can't have one missing.

I stare at her big stomach. "So, did you decide what you're going to name the baby?" I ask. Last week we got her talking about baby names for a full half hour of social studies.

"C'mon, Ally. No more stalling."

I don't answer.

"I mean it," she says, and I know she does.

I watch a mind movie of her taking a stick and drawing a line in the dirt between us under a bright blue sky. She's dressed as a sheriff and I'm wearing black and white prisoner stripes. My mind does this all the time—shows me these movies that seem so real that they carry me away inside of them. They are a relief from my real life.

I steel up inside, willing myself to do something I don't really want to do. To escape this teacher who's holding on and won't let go.

I pick up my pencil and her body relaxes, probably relieved that I've given in.

But, instead, knowing she loves clean desks and things just so, I grip my pencil with a hard fist. And scribble all over my desk.

"*Ally!*" She steps forward quick. "Why would you *do* that?"

The circular scribbles are big on top and small on the bottom. It looks like a tornado and I wonder if I meant to draw a picture of my insides. I look back up at her. "It was there when I sat down."

The laughter starts—but they're not laughing because they think I'm funny.

"I can tell that you're upset, Ally," Mrs. Hall says.

I am not hiding that as well as I need to.

"She's such a freak," Shay says in one of those loud whispers that everyone is meant to hear.

Oliver is drumming on his desk now.

"That's *it*," Mrs. Hall finally says. "To the office. *Now.*"

I wanted this but now I am having second thoughts.

"*Ally.*"

"Huh?"

Everyone laughs again. She puts up her hand. "Anyone

else who makes a sound gives up their recess." The room is quiet.

"Ally. I *said* to the office."

I can't go see our principal, Mrs. Silver, again. I go to the office so much, I wonder when they'll hang up a banner that says, "Welcome, Ally Nickerson!"

"I'm sorry," I say, actually meaning it. "I'll do it. I promise."

She sighs. "Okay, Ally, but if that pencil stops moving, you're *going*."

She moves me to the reading table next to a Thanksgiving bulletin board about being grateful. Meanwhile, she sprays my desk with cleaner. Glancing at me like she'd like to spray *me* with cleaner. Scrub off the dumb.

I squint a bit, hoping the lights will hurt my head less. And then I try to hold my pencil the way I'm supposed to instead of the weird way my hand wants to.

I write with one hand and shield my paper with the other. I know I better keep the pencil moving, so I write the word "Why?" over and over from the top of the page to the very bottom.

One, because I know how to spell it right and, two, because I'm hoping someone will finally give me an answer.

CHAPTER 2

Yellow Card

For Mrs. Hall's baby shower, Jessica shows up with such a big bunch of flowers from her father's florist shop that you'd swear she ripped a bush out of the ground and wrapped the bottom in foil.

Whatever. I don't care. I found a bright card with yellow roses at the store. And a picture of flowers won't dry up in a week. I feel like it's my way of saying I'm sorry for being such a pain all the time.

Max gives his present to Mrs. Hall. He leans back in his chair with his hands clasped behind his head as she opens it. He's given her diapers. I think he hoped to get a reaction from her and seems disappointed when she's happy.

Max likes attention. He also likes parties. Just about every day, he asks Mrs. Hall for a party and today, he's finally getting one.

When Mrs. Hall finally slides my card out of the envelope, she doesn't read it out loud like all the others. She hesitates and I know that she must really love it. And I feel proud, which isn't something I feel very much.

Our principal, Mrs. Silver, leans over to look. I figure I might finally get a compliment for once, but instead, her eyebrows bunch up and she motions me toward the door.

Shay has gotten up to look. She laughs and says, "The world gets dumber every time Ally Nickerson speaks."

"Shay. *Sit* down," Mrs. Hall says, but it's too late. You can't make people unhear something. I should be used to this, but it still takes a piece out of me every time.

As Shay and Jessica laugh I remember how we dressed up as our favorite book character for Halloween last week. I came as Alice in Wonderland, from the book my grandpa read to me a ton of times. Shay and her shadow, Jessica, called me Alice in Blunderland all day.

Keisha steps up to Shay and says, "Why don't you mind your own business for once?"

I like Keisha. She isn't afraid. And I'm afraid of so much.

Shay turns, looking like she's ready to swat a fly. "Like it's *your* business?" she asks her.

"That's right. It's *not* my business, but it's as much yours . . . as it is mine," Keisha replies.

Shay lets out a small gasp. "*Stop* talking to me."

"*Stop* being mean," Keisha replies, leaning forward.

Max folds his arms and leans forward across his desk. "*Yes*. There's going to be a fight," he says.

"There's *isn't* going to be a *fight*," Mrs. Hall says.

Suki is holding one of her small wooden blocks. She has a collection of them that she keeps in a box and I see her take one out when she gets nervous. She's nervous now.

Shay glares at Keisha. Keisha is new this year and I'm surprised she's said something.

Everyone is all riled up and I don't even know how this all happened.

While Mrs. Hall tells them both to cool off and points out to Max that it's foolish to root for a fight, Mrs. Silver waves me toward the door. What the heck is going on?

Once we're out in the hallway, I can tell by Mrs. Silver's face that it's going to be another one of those times when I'll have to say I'm sorry or explain why I've done something. The thing is, I have no idea why I'm even in trouble this time.

I stuff my hands in my pockets to keep them from doing something I'll regret. I wish I could put my mouth in there, too.

"I just don't get it, Ally," she says. "You've done other things that have been inappropriate, but this is just . . . well . . . *different*. It's not like you."

It figures; I do something *nice* and she says it isn't like me. And I can't understand how buying a card is bad.

"Ally," Mrs. Silver says. "If you're looking for attention, this isn't the way to do it."

She has that wrong. I need attention like a fish needs a snorkel.

The door swings all the way open, hitting the lockers, and Oliver springs from the room. "Ally," he says. "I think you gave her that card to tell her you're sorry she has to leave us to go have some dumb baby. She's probably really sad. I feel sorry for her, too."

What is he *talking* about?

"Oliver?" Mrs. Silver asks. "Is there a reason you're out here?"

"Yeah! I was going to . . . um . . . I was . . . going to go to the boys' room. Yeah. That's it." And off he runs.

"Can I just go now?" I blurt out, feeling like the job of just standing here is something I can't do for another second.

She shakes her head a bit as she speaks. "I just don't get why in the *world* you'd give a pregnant woman a sympathy card?"

Sympathy card? I think. And I think some more. And

then I remember. My mom sends those to people when someone they love dies. My stomach churns, wondering what Mrs. Hall must have thought.

"You do know what a sympathy card *is*, Ally, don't you?"

I should deny that I know, but I nod because I don't want to have to hear Mrs. Silver explain it. And besides, she'll think I'm even dumber than I am. If that's possible.

"Then why would you do such a thing?"

I stand tall, but everything inside shrinks. The thing is I feel real bad. I mean, I felt terrible when the neighbor's dog died, never mind if a baby had died. I just didn't know it was a sad card like that. All I could see were beautiful yellow flowers. And all I could imagine was how happy I was going to make her.

But there are piles of reasons I can't tell the absolute truth.

Not to her.

Not to anyone.

No matter how many times I have prayed and worked and hoped, reading for me is still like trying to make sense of a can of alphabet soup that's been dumped on a plate. I just don't know how other people do it.